SIT. STAY. LOVE. *Read. Enjoy!*

A DOGWOOD SWEET ROMANTIC COMEDY

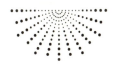

PAM MCCUTCHEON

[signature: Pam McCutcheon]

PARKER
HAYDEN
MEDIA

ISBN: 978-1-941528-89-1
Parker Hayden Media
5740 N. Carefree Circle, Ste 120-1
Colorado Springs, CO 80922

Art credits:
Cover Design: LB Hayden
Legs: Gpointstudio/DepositPhotos
Umbrella: Kurganov
Dog: Lifeonwhite/DepositPhotos

For all the dogs I've loved over the years:
Princess, Scottie, Lady, Meagan, Caitlin, Bonnie, Mo, Daisy, Abby,
and Trixie.

CHAPTER ONE

"I CAN'T BELIEVE they treated you like a dog," Katrina Channing fumed as she stalked back through the brisk autumn wind to her trailer. She glanced down at Lira, the famous Old English sheepdog. "Okay, technically, you are one, but you know what I mean. You're the star of the movie—they shouldn't be so mean to you."

And, also technically, it was Lira's trailer, not Kat's, since she was the headliner. "It's okay, sweetie," she told the lovable dog as she unlocked the door. "You did great today—no matter what they said."

So what if Lira had missed a few cues on set today? That was no reason for Edward to be so exasperated. Angry, even. Lira had done everything they needed her to do . . . eventually.

Kat took off her coat, opened the window a smidge to get some air into the stuffy trailer, and joined Lira on the floor where she'd flopped down on her huge dog bed. "You couldn't help it," she said, her voice thick as she gave Lira a hug. "You're just having a bad day. A bit of blurry vision, that's all. A break between movies will do you good."

Lira looked at her solemnly and nudged her with her nose, for all the world as if she were comforting Kat, instead of the other way around.

Kat brushed away a tear. Lira had been missing cues for days, and the on-call vet had told them that her deteriorating eyesight was probably incurable. To be certain of his diagnosis, he wanted them to bring Lira to an ophthalmology specialist next week for further examination. "They'll find a way to fix your vision, don't worry."

Lira sighed and dropped her head between her paws, her distinctive harlequin half-white, half-black facial markings prominent. She nosed a knotted rope toward Kat hopefully.

Kat grinned, but before she could accept Lira's invitation to play, her phone rang. She dug it out of her pocket, glanced at the caller ID, and groaned. *Mom*. She toyed with the idea of ignoring it, but knew her mother would just keep calling.

With resignation, she answered the phone. "Hi, Mom," she said brightly, hoping her mother would be in a pleasant mood for a change.

No such luck. Without even pausing for a greeting, her mother said, "Do you know what your father has done *now*?"

Nothing good, obviously. Gerald Channing couldn't do anything good in her mother's eyes. Kat sighed. "Why do you care, Mom? You've been divorced for twelve years." The divorce had been especially vicious, and neither one of her parents had ever gotten over it. They were still bitter, Mom especially. "You don't have to deal with him anymore. Unfriend him on Facebook and you won't even know what he's doing."

"Well, when you have a child together, it's necessary to communicate for the child's sake," her mother said indignantly.

"Well, as the only 'child' in question, I can tell you, it's better for me if you don't," Kat snapped back. Besides, that wasn't Eloise Channing's real motive anyway, though she wouldn't admit it. Kat's parents were so busy flinging accusations and trying to hurt each other that they really didn't even know what was going on in their child's life.

Kat reminded herself she liked it that way—she tried to avoid both of them as much as possible. "I really don't want to hear it, Mom."

"You're taking his side," Mom accused.

Kat's jaw tightened. "No, I'm trying very hard *not* to take sides or get involved." Though she wished they'd think about *her* side for a change. "And I really can't talk now—I have to get back to work."

"Work? What are you doing now?"

Was that a spark of maternal interest? "I told you a couple of weeks ago—I'm at Garden of the Gods filming—"

"You're in Colorado Springs?" her mother screeched. "Are you seeing your father?"

"No, Mom." He had a new family up in Denver now, and Kat didn't want to intrude. Besides, he was almost as bitter as Mom about the divorce and wouldn't let it go. "I'm here on a job—I'm working as an assistant to Edward Barton, the famous dog trainer, on a movie set."

"Well, you change jobs so often, I can't keep track of what you're doing or where you are. You flit from one job to another like a hummingbird. You're almost thirty—"

"I'm only twenty-eight," Kat corrected her.

"That's what I meant. You're old enough to settle down, don't you think?"

"I haven't found the right job yet," Kat protested. She really liked this one since it combined her love of movies and animals, but the way things were going, she didn't think Lira was going to be a hot commodity much longer.

"What about finding a husband, having babies?"

Oh, sure, then having a lovely divorce like her parents? "Someday," she hedged.

"Well, if you'd stick around in one job or one place for very long, you might meet the right person."

Kat rolled her eyes. That old refrain? She wasn't flighty—she just couldn't stand to be around toxic people. She'd rather quit a job when the people got too much to take than stick around and be miserable.

Before Kat could comment, her mother added, "Say, isn't your friend there in the Springs? That nice boy who used to live next door to us?"

"Mike Duffy?" For heaven's sake, she hadn't thought about him in years. She smiled, remembering the great times they'd had together. But they'd drifted apart after the Rat Incident.

"Yes—he's the one. Why don't you look him up while you're there? I'm friends with his mother on Facebook, and she posts about him every once in a while. He's still not married . . . and he's a doctor."

"He's a veterinarian," Kat corrected her. Besides, she didn't think Mike ever wanted to see her again.

"He's still a doctor, and you love animals. Think about it."

"Okay, Mom, I'll think about it. But for now, I gotta go. They want me back on the set," she lied.

"Okay, honey. ImissyouandIloveyou. Goodbye."

Kat made an affirmative noise and hung up. *Imissyouand-Iloveyou. Yeah, right.* She might believe it more if her mother didn't use the exact same refrain every time. As if it were a rote sentiment instead of something she actually felt.

Rubbing Lira's ears, she said, "Looks like we're both having a lousy day. It can't get much worse."

She grabbed one end of the knotted rope Lira had been hopefully offering, and engaged in a tug of war that made them both feel better.

The trailer door burst open and Joey Barton barged in.

Uh-oh, caught in the act. Again.

Kat looked up in chagrin to see his expression of disgust. She couldn't deny it—the evidence was overwhelming. There she stood, one end of the rope in her hand and the other end in the dog's mouth. "Don't you ever knock?" she demanded, hoping to put off whatever hateful thing he was about to say next.

"What do you think you're doing?" Joey demanded in his typical bellowing manner.

Kat decided to brazen it out. "What does it look like?"

He sneered. "It looks like you're playing with Lira again."

Lira pulled on the rope, trying to get Kat to resume their game of tug. "Yeah, so?"

"My uncle hired you to be Lira's assistant, not her playmate."

Kat let go of the rope and Lira dropped to the floor to gnaw on it. She might be the most famous canine star of all time, but she still liked to play. Kat raised her chin. "That's right, I'm an assistant, just like you."

Joey sneered again. "No, not like me. I'm assistant to an animal trainer—a man. You're nothing but a lackey to a mutt."

Self-important pig. Kat amended that thought. *No, that gives pigs a bad name. Make that pig dung.*

Besides, she was a pretty good at training dogs herself. But it was hard to get ahead in this competitive business, so when she saw that Edward Barton, the legendary Hollywood animal trainer, was looking for an assistant, she'd grabbed the chance. It was only temporary, but would look great on her résumé. Joey was a pain to work with, but for once, she was willing to put up with it because Lira was such a sweetheart and she was learning so much from Edward. She hoped he would ask her to continue on for Lira's next movie.

She glanced down at the big lovable dog. And if the job wasn't exactly what she'd been led to expect, so what? What was wrong with being Lira's assistant? Kat would far rather be her go-fer than play drudge to some petulant Hollywood human. At least Lira didn't make impossible demands. The dog only needed to be groomed, fed, and given a little love.

Besides, what she did with Lira was none of Joey's business. "Well, at least I'm good at *my* job."

Joey turned red and clenched his fists, then bit out, "Uncle Edward wants you to confirm the dog's eye appointment." Without waiting for her acknowledgment, he slammed out the door.

Kat sighed and silently berated herself. Why couldn't she learn to think first and speak later? Someday, her impulsiveness was going to get her into real trouble. She must have hit a little too close to home this time. Joey was lousy with animals, and everyone knew it—even him. He didn't understand animals, and they didn't like him. That didn't bode well for someone who aspired to take his uncle's place.

And Edward Barton was well-respected. He'd worked in relative obscurity, though, until he rescued Lira from the pound and shaped the sheepdog into box office gold. Though he was a wonderful trainer, Kat wished her boss had a little more compassion for the animals he owned and worked with. Oh, he was patient—usually—but he had no love for them and tended to treat them like hired hands instead of valued friends.

Kat had very definite feelings about how animals should be treated, and while the Bartons didn't abuse theirs, they didn't love them either. You could tell that by the dog's name —Lira, Italian for money. They saw her only as a cash cow. Well, a cash canine anyway.

Kat hugged her. Lira was so sweet-tempered, it was a shame she had to work so hard. Kat wished she could make the dog's life easier, but Edward didn't believe in spoiling his animals. So Kat rewarded her by allowing her to perform the one trick she loved above all others—the one cue she would respond to from anyone. Grinning, Kat shoved her fingers through her hair.

In delight, Lira sat back and let loose with one of her signature howls, known all over the world. "A-roo-roooo," she caroled.

Kat laughed and hugged her again, but Joey stuck his head back inside and growled, "Keep the dog quiet. They're filming."

He left but she didn't hear him move away. Wondering if he was staying close by to check up on her, Kat scratched the dog's ears. "It's okay, Lira, you did great."

Poor girl—what would happen to her if she went blind? She wouldn't be able to work, and that would be devastating for the attention-loving dog.

Outside the open window, Kat heard Joey hail his uncle in what he probably thought was a whisper. Joey, whose voice could double as a foghorn, couldn't whisper if his life depended on it. For heaven's sake, why was he being so secretive? Kat cracked the window open further so she could listen. So what if she was eavesdropping? This might affect Lira, not to mention her own livelihood.

". . . dog is totally worthless," Joey said.

Kat gritted her teeth. He was the one who was worthless. Lira was the one paying his salary, the idiot.

"Not totally," Edward said. "She's still the best animal I've ever trained, not to mention the one who's made me the most money. Don't knock it—she paid for your college education."

Ha! Take that, Joey.

"Sure, sure," Joey agreed like the brown-noser he was. "But your skills paid for my education, not the dog's. You're the best in the business. And don't think I don't appreciate what you've done for me. I do. Without you, I'd be nothing. I'd do anything for you. Anything."

Good grief, didn't the guy have any self-respect?

"That's okay," Edward said. "I helped you because your father would've wanted me to. And if you really want to repay me—"

"I do, I do."

"Then just continue learning, ask questions, and help me with the animals. And try to control your fear of mice. We'll be working with them on the next film."

Kat grinned as Joey muttered something incomprehensible. That was one fear she doubted he'd ever master. Joey was irrational when it came to rodents.

Edward continued. "You might also try to learn a little more . . . subtlety where people and animals are concerned. Do you understand what I mean?"

"Sure," Joey said.

Yeah, right. Subtlety wasn't Joey's strong suit. She doubted he understood what the word meant.

"No problem," Joey promised. "So what are you going to do about Lira?"

"If her blindness is incurable, there's nothing we can do."

"What about her upcoming contracts?"

Edward sighed. "I guess we'll have to cancel them."

"And lose all that money?"

"What other choice is there? It would be easy enough to disguise another dog to look like her, but most sheepdogs are difficult to train. I doubt I'll ever be able to find another like her. No, I guess we just have to forfeit the money."

"Don't you have insurance for this kind of thing?" Joey asked.

"No. I'm insured against her loss by death or accident, but not disease."

"So . . . the dog is worth more dead than alive?"

Edward gave a bark of laughter. "I guess you could say that."

"So what are you going to do?"

"Me? Nothing." He clapped Joey on the shoulder. "But you can help me out."

"How?"

"I'm going out of town for a few days. Why don't you put that college education of yours to work, and see if you can come up with a way for us to collect on that insurance policy, okay?"

"Okay," Joey agreed enthusiastically.

Edward said good-bye and Kat heard him walk away.

"Don't worry," Joey called after him. "I'll take care of it." He lowered his voice when Edward was out of earshot. "Subtlety, huh? I'm not stupid. I get it. I'll take care of Lira, all right."

Kat froze. She replayed the conversation in her mind. Had Edward just asked Joey to kill Lira for the insurance money? No, he couldn't have. Could he?

No, Joey must have misunderstood. She'd just go to Edward and—

And what? What if that *was* what Edward meant? She couldn't afford to let them know she'd overheard. And she certainly couldn't afford to leave either one of them alone with the dog until she was absolutely sure they didn't mean her any harm. Lira was the important thing. Kat had to protect Lira.

CHAPTER TWO

LIRA WAS GNAWING AWAY on her favorite toy, oblivious to the fact that her owner wanted her dead. Kat fumed. They would destroy a helpless dog just because she couldn't see as well as she used to?

What if the vet was wrong? Kat didn't put much store in the man's cursory examination. And she didn't trust any vet specialist he'd recommend. Surely another one would've done a better job—like Mike Duffy for instance.

Mike was the best friend she'd ever had. Kat and Mike, everyone had called them, the Irish twins. Kat wasn't Irish, and they weren't twins, but that didn't seem to matter. They'd been inseparable, even if Mike had always berated her for her impulsiveness.

She sure would like to see him again. And it had been at least eight years. Surely he'd forgiven her by now.

She snapped her fingers in sudden realization. Of course. That was it—she'd take Lira to Mike for a second opinion. If she could prove to Edward and Joey that there was a cure for Lira's vision loss, then there would be no need for them to hurt her. And no need to confirm the other eye appointment.

Kat pulled out her cell phone and looked up the number for Mike's practice. She called, but he was busy with a patient, so she made an appointment. Luckily, they had one right away.

But . . . how was she going to manage getting off the lot? It wasn't as if she could put sunglasses and a hat on the distinctive-looking dog and hope she'd go unnoticed—especially in Kat's car, a lime-green Volkswagen bug.

There was no time to disguise the dog—Kat would just have to brazen it out. But, in case they had to keep Lira overnight to fix her vision, she'd better take Lira's things with her. She grabbed the dog's collar, leash, grooming supplies, toys, and food, then grabbed her own overnight bag. "Lira, you want to go for a ride?"

The dog's ears perked up and she responded as Kat knew she would, with an enthusiastic woof and a wag of her short, stubby tail.

"Come on, then, let's go." Kat normally obtained Edward's permission to take Lira off the lot, but this time she didn't dare ask. The guards were used to her taking the dog out, so she'd take the chance they wouldn't hassle her.

She led Lira out to her car and put her in the back seat, tossing her paraphernalia in the trunk. The dog sat in her favorite position, right behind the driver's seat, with her head hanging out the window.

Suddenly, Lira growled, and Kat glanced up to see Joey entering the parking lot. Quickly, she said, "Down, girl," and gave her the proper cue, pointing at the floorboards. Obedient as always, Lira lay down out of sight, and Kat hopped in the car, then started it.

She kept her eyes averted, hoping to avoid making eye contact. She couldn't afford to halt with Lira in the car and didn't want to make Joey suspicious by not stopping if he waved her over. She steered her car to the exit and smiled at the guard.

"A bit breezy today," he said. "I hear we're in for some snow."

It would have to be the guard who liked to chat. Kat cursed silently, wishing she could just blow out of there. But that was the surest way to arouse his suspicions. "It's that time of year," she agreed.

He chuckled. "And I know how much Lira loves her rides—"

A shout came behind her and Kat grimaced. Joey.

"What's he want?" the guard asked, a frown on his face.

In sudden inspiration, Kat said, "Me, I guess. He's been pestering me ever since I started working for his uncle. I can't seem to get rid of him."

It wasn't a lie. Joey *was* a pest—just not in the way she'd implied.

She looked in the rearview mirror. Joey was in his car, and had his head out the window, waving at them. "Oh, no. He's headed this way."

The guard smiled. "That's all right, Miss. You go on. I'll hold him off."

He opened the gate and Kat shot through, relieved to be gone. She risked another glance in the rearview mirror and saw Joey gesticulating at the guard. Damn, he must have discovered Lira was missing. She only wished she'd asked the guard not to mention the dog's presence. Oh, well, too late now.

She released Lira from her stay position and the dog rose to hang her head out of the car, an expression of doggie bliss on her face as the wind blew through her hair. It would be hell to comb out later, but Lira was enjoying herself so much, Kat didn't mind. At a stoplight, she quickly texted Edward. *Lira sick. Taking her to vet. Be back soon.* There, maybe that would keep him from getting angry. Maybe he'd even call Joey off.

She checked the GPS and drove north to Mike's veterinarian practice in Briargate.

Though Lira didn't really need the restraint, Kat leashed her, then entered the office Mike shared with three other vets, whose names were all listed on the sign outside. The interior was quite nice, with spotlessly clean floors, attractive wooden benches, and a curving counter with several receptionists sitting behind it. Mike was doing very well for himself.

There were a few people in the waiting room and one little boy's eyes grew huge and round when he spotted Lira.

Damn. Kat had forgotten to warn the receptionist ahead of time that the famous dog star was coming so they could avoid the waiting room and the fawning adoration Lira caused everywhere she went.

"Look, Mommy," the little boy said. "It's Lira."

"Don't be silly," his mother started to say, then paused when she got a good look at the dog. She looked up at Kat. "*Is* that Lira?"

There was no disguising the dog's distinctive markings, so Kat nodded.

"It is not," another boy scoffed.

"Is too," the first one said.

A fight looked imminent, so Kat interrupted. "Yes, it really is Lira. Watch."

She caught the dog's attention and shoved her fingers through her hair. Immediately, Lira howled, "A-roo-roooo." The sound echoed in the small office.

The children laughed in delight. "It *is* Lira," the Doubting Thomas declared and both boys came over to lavish attention on the dog.

A man poked his head out into the hallway from one of the examining rooms. "What's that noise?" he demanded.

One of the receptionists chuckled. "It's Lira, sir." When he didn't look enlightened, she added, "The famous dog star?"

"I see. Well, keep her quiet, will you?"

"Yes, Dr. Duffy."

Dr. Duffy? Mike? It *was* him. "Hey, Mikey, remember me?"

Mike winced at the hated nickname, then his eyes widened. "Kat?"

That's all the encouragement she needed. She ran down the hall and barreled into his arms, giving him a big bear hug. "Yes, it's me. How *are* you?"

Mike returned her hug, then, noting their very interested audience, peeled her off with a raised eyebrow. "Still the same old Kat, I see. Always impulsive."

"And you're the same old Mike—a stick-in-the-mud." That wasn't entirely true. Now that she'd gotten a good look at him, she realized her old pal Mikey had changed. The thin frame she remembered had expanded to a pair of impressive shoulders and a nice physique. Not only that, but his face had cleared up, and he'd gotten a decent haircut.

Instead of the geeky, rather endearing guy she remembered, Mike had turned into quite a hottie. With his open face, wide smile, and beautiful blue eyes beneath tousled brown hair, he looked like the boy next door.

Kat grinned. Of course, he *had* been the boy next door—from the time they were eight until her mother had moved her to California when she was sixteen after the divorce. She'd moved back to Colorado ten years ago, when she'd turned eighteen and had come back to attend college with him.

Mike glanced around at their audience, still avidly

watching their every move. "I, uh, can't talk right now. I have patients—"

"I know," Kat said. "I'm next."

"You are?"

"Well, the dog is."

Mike turned toward the receptionist who had recognized Lira. She nodded, smiling.

He looked confused and shoved a hand through his already disheveled hair in an habitual gesture Kat remembered well. "Uh, sure. Where's your patient?"

Kat looked back into the waiting room. Lira wasn't paying any attention to them. Instead, she was engaged in licking the face of one delighted, giggling boy and "shaking hands" with another. Kat chuckled. She hated to drag Lira away from her adoring public, but . . .

"Lira," she called. The dog looked up, and Kat made a broad "come" gesture, big enough for the dog to see.

Lira bounded over, and Mike led them into a nearby examining room. He knelt to give the dog a scratch behind the ear, saying, "What do we have here?"

Kat smiled down at him, saying softly, "It's good to see you again, Mike."

Mike averted his gaze, seemingly engrossed in examining Lira. "It's nice to see you, too, Kat. But I don't have time to chat—I have a lot of appointments today, and I don't like to keep anyone waiting. What can I help you with?"

She felt a pang of disappointment. Why was Mike so cold? Did he still blame her for the Rat Incident? That was eight years ago. Up until then, they'd been best friends. Had one mistake erased all that? Ignoring his last question, she asked, "Well, let's have dinner, then, to talk over old times."

Mike hesitated, and Kat added, "I'm going to bug you until you say yes, you know."

He looked up at her then and grinned. "I know. Okay, dinner. But first, tell me why you brought Lira to see me."

Kat rubbed the dog's ears. "She's losing her vision. I was hoping you could examine her, tell me what we need to do to cure her."

"I see." Mike bent down to peer in Lira's eyes. "Hmm. Sheepdogs are usually prone to cataracts, but I don't see any. When did you first notice her vision problem?"

"She's been missing cues for a couple of weeks."

"Cues?"

"Yes. Lira's an actor."

"I see." Mike sounded disinterested. He would be. He'd always been far more interested in animals' health and well-being than their monetary value. "Have you noticed any decrease in night vision?"

Kat thought about it. "Hmm, now that you mention it, lately she seems to be reluctant to go outside in the dark—as if she's afraid. And when we do go out, she sticks real close to me."

Mike nodded. "I thought so."

"What? What is it?"

"Wait here. I have to check something." He left, then returned with an instrument he used to examine Lira's eyes.

Soon, he set the tool down and turned to Kat with a compassionate expression.

She knew that look. Mike had bad news. "What?" she asked.

Mike patted the dog. "I'm afraid Lira probably has PRA."

"What's that?"

"Progressive retinal atrophy—a gradual wasting or thinning of the retina. But a specialist could give you more information."

Her gut churned. That must be what the on-call vet meant. "You can cure it, right?"

Regret filled his eyes. "No, I'm afraid not. It's incurable. Lira is going blind."

Stunned, Kat sat down in a nearby chair and tried to take it all in. Lira was really going blind? She buried her hands in the thick fur at the dog's neck, blinking away the stinging tears that threatened to overflow her eyes. In a thick voice, she asked, "Are you sure?"

As Lira licked her face in an attempt to console her, Mike said, "Well, an ophthalmologist—"

"No. Tell me what *you* think." She trusted him far more, and knew he'd give it to her straight.

"Yes, Kat, I'm sure. It's pretty far along. I'm sorry, there's nothing anyone can do."

"But . . . but Lira can't work without her eyesight. She's been trained with mostly visual cues."

Mike remained silent as Kat's mind raced, trying to find a solution. "Unless . . . we could retrain her using verbal cues. That would work, wouldn't it?"

"Maybe. But how could she follow them if she can't see?"

He had a point. Lira wouldn't be able to see where she was going or what she was doing. In desperation, Kat rose to clutch Mike's sleeve. "Please, you've got to find a way to cure her. If you don't, she's dead."

"I'm sorry, there's no cure. But the disease isn't fatal. She'll live, she just won't be able to see. Many dogs cope quite well—"

"No, you don't understand," Kat explained urgently. "If Lira's blindness is incurable, then she's in grave danger."

Mike's expression took on a wary edge. "Danger?"

"Yes. She's a very valuable dog, and if she can't work, she's no use to Edward—her trainer. His nephew Joey will kill her to collect the insurance money. That's canine homicide. Or caninicide . . . dogicide?"

"Now, Kat—"

17

"No, really. It's true. I overheard Edward telling Joey to murder Lira."

Mike rubbed the back of his neck and gave her a doubtful look. "You *heard* him say this?"

"Well, not in so many words, but he certainly implied it, and I know that's how Joey took it." She paused, seeing she wasn't getting through. "Mike, please. You gotta believe me. Lira's life is in danger and I need your help."

Mike regarded her with a serious expression, as if weighing her words, then said, "No, Kat, not this time."

Her jaw dropped. Oh, no. If her oldest and dearest friend wouldn't help her, who would?

CHAPTER THREE

THE DISAPPOINTMENT on Kat's face was almost too much to bear. When she gazed up at Mike with those big blue eyes framed by a mop of white-blond hair, she looked like Kaley Cuoco—adorably so. He found her hard to resist, but he couldn't get involved with one of her crazy schemes again.

The dog settled down, nose between her paws, as Kat pierced him with a look. "Why won't you help me?"

He avoided her gaze as he sought for a way to explain. Ever since he and Kat had parted, his life had been smooth, predictable. No late-night demands for help with some bizarre plot, no run-ins with the law, no surprises. He liked it that way.

"Because your weird logic is insidious," he explained. "It sneaks up on you, making everything sound so reasonable . . . right up until you're blindsided by the truth."

He ought to know—he'd been caught unaware often enough.

"I see," Kat said stiffly. "You still haven't forgiven me for the Rat Incident."

On the contrary, he could forgive her anything. That was

part of the problem. But he couldn't forget the way she turned his life upside down. "Could you blame me if I hadn't?"

Kat bristled in self-defense. "I had good reasons for holding those rats hostage. The school administration wouldn't meet my demands."

He gave her an exasperated look. "But did you have to barricade yourself in *my* lab to do it?"

"I had to do something to make them listen. I thought if I held the rats hostage . . ." She gave him a sheepish glance. "I guess it didn't work, huh?"

"Obviously. Did you really think the school would agree to find good homes for them?"

"Sure. Why not?"

"They were lab rats, not pets."

"But they *experimented* on them."

"Would you rather we experimented on people?"

With a glare, she said, "Even rats deserve humane treatment."

"Well, they've got it now. Since you let them go, the school's infested with their descendants—their very *smart* descendants. They've even named them after you—Kat's Rats."

"After me?" she said in a small voice.

"Yes, it's become a challenge for each new class to figure out how to get rid of them."

Kat's look of dismay was almost comical. "I-I thought they'd run for the hills."

"That's the problem," he said gently. "You leap in, guns blazing, and never think about the consequences."

She bit her lip. "I didn't mean to get you in trouble."

And she wouldn't have if he hadn't stupidly lent her his lab key. But he wasn't going to get sucked into another one of her crazy plots. "Don't worry about it. They decided not to kick me out. I still graduated."

She brightened. "Yes, and everything turned out just fine. See?"

He shook his head. Only Kat would see anything positive in that incident. "But it could have turned out very badly," he reminded her.

Kat gazed at him earnestly. "This is different. This time it's real and very serious. If you don't help me, Lira could die."

"With you, it's always serious—"

"Dr. Duffy?" his receptionist said, poking her head in the door.

In relief, he turned to her. "I'm sorry, Aimee. This appointment is taking longer than I expected."

She gave him a knowing look, though his matchmaking receptionist appeared a bit disappointed that she hadn't caught them in each others' arms again. "That's okay. You have a cancellation. But Clarence escaped again, and there's a very insistent man in the waiting room with a . . . problem."

"What kind of problem?"

"I don't know. He doesn't have an animal with him and refuses to tell me what's wrong. Will you talk to him?"

"Yes, of course." He turned to Kat. "I'm sorry, but—"

"That's okay. Who's Clarence?"

"The clinic's pet mouse. He fancies himself an escape artist and enjoys making us chase him around the room before he deigns to return to his cage." He quirked an eyebrow. "Just like one of Kat's Rats."

She made a face at him.

He grinned. "It might take a while, so—"

"No problem, I'll just wait here."

"But—"

"Our conversation isn't over yet," she said mulishly.

He cast around for help. "We might need this room."

"No, we won't," Aimee informed him in an irritatingly perky manner. "Not for another hour or so."

Exasperated, Mike ran his hand through his hair. A sudden howling, "A-roo-roooo," had him spinning around to stare at the dog. She sat there, gazing up at him, her tongue lolling out in delight.

He glanced at Kat. "Does she do that often?"

Kat shrugged. "Anytime you make that gesture. It's her cue to howl, her trademark."

"What gesture?"

She pointed at his hand, halfway to his forehead again. "That. Running your fingers through your hair. She can still see broad movements."

He hesitated, hand frozen in the act, and glanced down at Lira. Sure enough, the dog watched him with an intent expression, just waiting for an opportunity to let loose again. He dropped his hand and could swear Lira's face fell. "I see."

With both women watching him in amusement, he had no choice but to stage a strategic retreat. Turning to Aimee, he asked, "Where's the man with the problem?"

"In the waiting room."

"And Clarence was in room two?"

"Right."

"Then show the man in there so I can look for Clarence while I hear him out."

Mike washed his hands before joining the "problem" and opened the door to room two carefully, staring down at the floor. This time, Clarence didn't take advantage of the opening to make a break for it, but there was a small, twitchy man inside, eyeing the mouse cage nervously. Mike closed the door behind him and glanced around, but didn't see Clarence. "How can I help you?"

The man gave him an insincere smile and spoke in a loud voice. "Thank you for giving me your time."

"Certainly. What can I do for you?" Surreptitiously, Mike checked out the baseboards. No Clarence.

"You have a girl here with a large sheepdog. Don't deny it. I followed her here, and I just heard the dog howl."

Mike raised an eyebrow. "I have no intention of denying it." He peered behind the objects on the counter. No white mouse.

"Good. Is there some way you can keep them here another few minutes while I explain?"

"They're not going anywhere. Why?" Mike asked, though he had a sinking feeling he didn't want to know the answer.

Apparently relieved, the man stuck out his hand. "I'm Joey Barton—the owner of that sheepdog. The girl stole it."

Mike groaned inwardly. He should have known. Temporarily abandoning the search for Clarence, he motioned toward a chair. "All right, Mr. Barton—"

"Just call me Joey."

"Joey, then. Why don't you sit down and tell me about it."

"Do you know who Lira is?"

"Yes, Miss Channing told me."

"Then you know how valuable she is."

"In my clinic, all animals are equal."

"Of course, of course. But this dog is worth a lot of money to my uncle."

"Your uncle? I thought the dog was yours."

Joey looked startled. "It is. I mean, uh, my uncle and I train animals together so Lira belongs to both of us."

"I see. And your point is?"

"Kat is the dog's assistant, but she's not supposed to remove her from the lot without permission. I saw her sneak off and I followed them here. She's obviously stolen the dog. Will you help me get it back?"

Stealing didn't sound like Kat . . . unless she thought it was for a good cause, of course, like averting potential "dogicide."

Whatever. Mike brought his mind back to the subject at hand. Hedging, he asked, "Why would she do that?"

"Who knows? She's such a ditz, she probably thought she could sell the dog and no one would notice Lira is the most famous dog in the world."

Mike frowned. He didn't like this guy's attitude. "She thinks you want to kill the dog."

Joey's eyes opened wide. "K-kill the dog? Why would I want to do that?"

He was so obviously surprised that Mike had to concede he was probably telling the truth. Besides, Kat had made many a mountain out of misinterpreted molehills. No doubt this was just another one of her misunderstandings.

"Okay," Mike said. "Wait here." He paused with his hand on the doorknob. "Oh, and don't open the door. There's a mouse on the loose."

"M-mouse?"

"Is that a problem? I thought you worked with animals."

Joey gave him a sickly smile. "No, n-no problem. Uh, but hurry, willya?"

Mike found Kat in the room where he'd left her. She and the dog both looked up at him expectantly. "Mike, you gotta—"

"No," he said firmly. "Barton is here for his dog."

"Edward is here?"

"No, Joey."

Incredulously, Kat said, "Joey?" At Mike's nod, she continued, "How'd he find me?"

"He followed you."

Kat grabbed Lira's leash. "Thanks for telling me. I'll sneak out the back—"

"That won't solve anything."

"What?"

"Think about it. Don't you think it's possible you might have misunderstood something he said? After all, it's happened before."

"I know, but this time it's for real. If I don't stop him, he'll kill Lira for the insurance."

"You said yourself that he didn't actually *say* that. Don't you think you might be mistaken?"

"Not this time, Mike," she said with a stubborn look.

Mike sighed. She believed she was completely in the right. But then, she always did. This time he wasn't going to let her protests sway him. "I can't let you take this dog from her rightful owner."

"Didn't you hear me?" she demanded. "I said he's going to murder her. How can you let him do that?" When Mike said nothing, her annoyance turned to incredulity. "You don't believe me. You think I'm lying."

"No, I think you're mistaken."

"Well, you're wrong. And I'm *not* turning this dog over to Joey."

Mike shot a wary glance at Lira, managing to stop himself before he raked his hand through his hair again. "All right. How about this? We'll call the police."

"So they can arrest me? No thanks."

He made a calming gesture with his hands. "No, so they can sort this out. They'll see you made an honest mistake and let you go. And if you're right, Lira will be protected."

"I don't know. . . ."

"I do," Mike said firmly. "Wait here, and I'll call them."

He closed the door on Kat, leaving her chewing her lower lip and looking thoughtful. He went back to room two and found Joey darting glances all around the room, jittering in impatience. He looked up when Mike came in. "Well?"

"She won't turn the dog over to you."

Joey's face reddened. "Then I'll call the police and have her arrested." Though his words were fierce, his gaze still darted around the room.

"That won't be necessary," Mike explained. "I'll call them myself and have them straighten this out."

"The . . . the police?" Joey looked taken aback. "I didn't mean it. I mean, if we can just have the dog back, I won't press charges."

Relieved, Mike said, "Glad to hear it, but this is the best way to settle it for both of you." His eyes narrowed in sudden suspicion. "Unless there's a reason you don't want to call them?"

Joey backtracked. "No, no. Please, call them. I just didn't want to make this difficult."

He saw no reason not to believe the man, especially given Kat's history. Satisfied by Joey's explanation, Mike nodded and left. Joey tried to follow but Mike stopped him. "It would be better if you stayed here. I don't want the clinic disrupted any more than it already is."

"Here? But—"

"Do you have a problem with that?"

"Oh, no," Joey assured him, though his uneasy gaze swept the room again.

Shaking his head, Mike left to make the call. The bored policeman on the other end of the phone promised to send someone right away, and Mike went back to work until they arrived.

About half an hour later, Aimee called him aside to tell him she'd shown the policeman into the same room with Joey. Mike joined them.

"Did Mr. Barton explain the situation?" he asked the police officer.

"Yes, but I understand there's another side to the story.

Can I see Miss . . ." he checked his notes, ". . . Miss Channing?"

"Of course," Mike said. The presence of this no-nonsense type was just what Kat needed to see how foolish she was acting. "She's in the other room."

Joey shoved open the door, saying, "Which room?"

Mike caught a flurry of movement out of the corner of his eye. Damn. Clarence had made a break for it. Now they'd never find him. But Mike didn't have time to worry about that now.

Gesturing toward the other examining room, he said, "They're in here." He opened the door, staring inside in disbelief. Kat was gone.

Joey pushed past him. "Where is she?"

"I don't know. She was here a moment ago. Aimee?" The receptionist came over. "Did you see Miss Channing leave?"

"No," she answered. "She didn't pass my desk." She pointed toward the end of the hallway. "She must have gone out the back way."

Joey ran to open the door at the end of the hall and glanced around. He whirled, bellowing. "She's gone. You let her get away."

Mike's jaw tightened. Kat might be in the wrong, but this guy had no right to act as though she were a hardened criminal. "I didn't *let* her do anything. She made that decision on her own."

"See?" Joey yelled at the police officer. "Doesn't that prove she's guilty?"

"Not necessarily," Mike interrupted. "According to her, you're the guilty one, with plans to kill the dog to collect the insurance."

Joey sputtered. "B-but that's ridiculous—"

"Mr. Barton," Mike interrupted with far more politeness

than he felt, "I'll have to ask you to keep your voice down. You're upsetting the patients."

Joey's expression hardened into belligerence. "You—" He broke off, a look of horror on his face. Then suddenly, he performed a mad stomping dance down the length of the hall-way, his arms flailing as he screeched, "No, no, get it off me!"

What the heck? Mike watched in astonishment as Joey started beating on himself, waling away at his right leg. When he stood still long enough, Mike saw a small lump under Joey's trousers rapidly traverse his thigh. Clarence!

Mike tried to stifle his laughter as Aimee went to the mouse's rescue. "Be still," she ordered. "You'll hurt Clarence."

Still wiggling like a landed fish, Joey goggled at her in disbelief. "Me hurt *him?*" His eyes widened and he suddenly started capering again. "He's on my butt." He tore at his belt. "Oh, no, he's headed for my crotch!"

By now, he'd drawn a small audience of giggling bystanders. Even the policeman had dropped his cool facade and was snickering with the rest of them.

"Stop that," Aimee said, trying to help. "If you'll just stand still—"

"Forget that," Joey exclaimed, then ripped his zipper open and dropped his pants. For the sake of the children in the audience, Mike was glad to see he wore boxer shorts, though his choice seemed a little odd—a grinning SpongeBob in his square pants.

Clarence must have liked them too, for he scurried up one of the legs. A look of pure horror came over Joey's face as he pulled his waistband out and stared inside, still gyrating madly.

Aimee, obviously concerned about Clarence, said, "Here, let me help." She reached inside Joey's boxers and grabbed.

He yelped.

"Oops," Aimee said, grinning. "I don't think that was Clarence. Too small."

Joey gave her an indignant glare, but the audience roared with laughter. Aimee grabbed again. "Got him," she said in triumph, and pulled the mouse out of Joey's underwear. Clarence wiggled his whiskers, and Mike swore the mouse had a smirk on his face. It matched the one on everyone else's.

With his pants still around his ankles and SpongeBob quivering in indignation, Joey yelled, "That's not funny."

Everyone just laughed harder. Joey yanked his pants on and fastened them. Casting a dirty look at the laughing crowd, he said, "Come on, let's finish this somewhere else."

Mike and the policeman followed him back into the examining room, both trying hard to stifle their chuckles.

Joey whirled on the officer. "So you think this is funny, do you?"

The cop grinned. "Well, yes."

"You won't think it's so funny when I have your job," Joey threatened.

The cop sobered, though a small smile played around his mouth. "Why? Because I didn't dive into your shorts to rescue you from an itty bitty mouse?"

Mike covered his mouth to hide his smile.

Joey shivered in revulsion, but said, "No, forget the mouse. I'm talking about Lira."

"If you'll come down to the station and file a report, we'll see what we can do."

"You'll see what you can do?" Joey mimicked. "I'm afraid that's not good enough. You need to find her *now*."

The officer's expression turned enigmatic. "We'll get to it as soon as we can." But from the look on his face, a dognapping wasn't going to be a high priority.

Joey must have made the same interpretation, for he said, "You don't understand. This dog is *Lira*."

"Lira?"

"The world-famous dog star. You, know, star of *Lira Takes Manhattan*, *Lira Loves London*?"

Comprehension dawned on the cop's face.

Joey stabbed a finger at him to stress his point. "And what about your recent campaign to appear a kinder, gentler police force?" he sneered. "How would you like to be known as the department who let a maniac kidnap the most famous dog in the world? There are a lot of children who are going to be very upset if you let that happen—not to mention their parents."

Joey's threats seemed to work, though the officer didn't appear to appreciate his methods. Snapping his notebook shut, he said, "We'll see what we can do."

Joey bounced on the balls of his feet, apparently satisfied.

Concerned, Mike interjected, "You will wait to hear Kat's side, won't you?"

"Kat?" Joey said suspiciously. "You know her?"

"Yes," Mike admitted. "She's an old friend."

"Then you're not exactly unbiased, are you?" Joey asked.

"I assure you—"

"Of course we'll listen to both sides," the officer said with a reassuring look. "But taking off like that doesn't do her much good. You'll both get the chance to tell your stories, but we need Mr. Barton to come down to the station and file charges."

"No problem," Joey said, his volume rising again. "Let me just call my office and I'll be right there." He glanced down at his cell phone. "Is there somewhere I can talk *privately*?"

Mike was reluctant to have this loudmouth in his clinic any longer than necessary, but couldn't find a good reason to deny him. The best Mike could do was show Joey into the tiny office behind the reception area. At least there he could talk at the top of his lungs without bothering too many people.

Mike escorted the policeman out, then called in his next patient and tried to put the incident out of his mind. Kat wasn't his responsibility and he couldn't get involved in her problems again. Unfortunately, it was difficult not to. They'd been a part of each others' lives for so many years, ever since he'd moved in next door to her.

Even then, she'd been a loose cannon. Oh, she didn't mean to cause trouble, but it just naturally followed her. He smiled to himself. Kat was many things, including flaky, but she was also generous and kind.

She'd been his best friend. More tomboy than girl, Kat had joined in all the rough and tumble games he enjoyed, and had generously shared her loving dog Goldie with the lonely new kid on the block.

Their friendship had continued over the years, his evolving into an adolescent crush, then into love when she developed into a beautiful woman. Kat never noticed. She still regarded him as the geeky boy next door, the childhood playmate who could always be counted on to get her out of scrapes—after she conned him into participating in them, of course.

But no more. He'd given up long ago on hoping she'd see him as anything more than a friend, and had spent the intervening years getting over her and building a life for himself.

He'd done a good job of it, too. He had a good practice, a comfortable home, and plenty of dates. None of them had evolved into a serious relationship, but he hadn't given up hope. And he didn't want to jeopardize his comfortable life for the upheaval and pain Kat left in her wake.

So why was he thinking about her so much? Resolutely,

he put her out of his mind, and escorted the patient out of the examining room. Aimee met him, looking anxious.

"What's wrong?" he asked.

She crossed her hands over her stomach. "I just . . . overheard something I think you ought to know, especially since Miss Channing is a friend of yours."

"Overheard?"

"Yes. I didn't really mean to," she said in a rush, "but Mr. Barton was so loud I couldn't help it."

He could believe that. "Why are you so upset?"

"He was leaving a voicemail, kinda gloating about what just happened."

Suddenly apprehensive, Mike nodded at her to continue.

"He bragged that he'd found Lira and how he was going to 'off her,' then blame it on Miss Channing."

"Are you sure about this?"

"Yes. He said they'd be able to collect the insurance when the dog was dead."

Mike clenched his fists against a sudden onslaught of anger. "Where is he?"

She gestured helplessly. "He's gone. He left right after he hung up."

Though his adrenaline surged, seeking some sort of outlet, Mike nodded and managed to say, "That's all right, don't worry about it."

"Will you tell Miss Channing?"

His adrenaline spiked again. Dear Lord, Kat was right for a change . . . and he'd blown her off. Damn. Not only had he not believed her, but he'd made it worse by calling the police in.

I'm a fool. But how could he know that, for once in her life, Kat hadn't blown everything out of proportion?

"Dr. Duffy?" Aimee asked tentatively, interrupting his self-flagellation.

"Yes?"

"Are you going to tell Miss Channing?"

"Yes, of course—" He stopped, realizing he didn't have her phone number. How was he going to warn her? "No, damn it. I don't have her number."

"You don't?" Aimee looked incredulous.

"No. This is the first time I've seen her in years. She didn't get a chance to give it to me before she . . . left." Before he'd screwed up so badly she had to flee. Though she'd asked him to have dinner with her, he figured she would have changed her mind after he didn't support her. "Didn't you get it?"

"She only gave me her work number."

"Then call them to get her cell number . . . or call information, wherever you need, just find her. And when you do, let me talk to her."

"What if I can't reach her?"

"Leave a message. Tell her it's urgent she call me here or at home." *I have an apology to make.*

An hour later, Aimee came in waving a piece of paper as if she'd found a winning lottery ticket. "I found her cell phone number!"

Relief flooded through him. "Good job." Eagerly, Mike dialed the number, but it went to voicemail. He left a message for Kat to call right away, and checked with Aimee each time the phone rang, but no Kat. He somehow made it through the rest of the day, chastising himself and calling himself twenty-three kinds of a fool. When he finished with his last patient, he went to find Aimee. "Any word?"

She shook her head, a look of concern on her face.

"Don't worry about it," he said. This mess wasn't her fault. "You've done all you can. I'll continue trying to call her tonight. I'm sure I'll reach her." He said the words for Aimee's benefit, but he had no such confidence. He'd really messed up this time.

As he drove home, he couldn't help but worry. Not only about what would happen to Kat, but the dog, too. Lira might be going blind, but that wouldn't degrade her quality of life. She had quite a few healthy, happy years ahead of her. It would be a pity to destroy the animal simply because she was unable to follow a few cues in front of a camera.

If Mike could help it, he wouldn't let Joey kill her—not for a stupid reason like that. Hell, he couldn't think of *any* reason good enough to justify putting down a healthy, well-adjusted dog.

He parked in the garage and went in the side door, tossing his keys on a nearby table. The rapid clicking sounds puzzled him until he looked up to see ninety pounds of shaggy sheepdog loping toward him. He barely had time to widen his eyes as the dog became airborne, then slammed into him.

Mike went down for the count. As he lay sprawled on the floor, stunned and trying to catch his breath, Lira held him down with one paw on each shoulder, her weight crushing his chest. She pinned him with her gaze and snarled, her teeth only inches from his exposed throat.

Mike froze. Maybe there *was* such a thing as justifiable dogicide.

CHAPTER FOUR

KAT STOOD in shock as Lira growled down at Mike. "Down, girl," she directed. "Off!" Neither cue did any good. Then, realizing the significance of the dog's action, she yelled, "Cut," and made a slicing gesture across her throat.

Lira ceased growling and gave Mike a big slurping kiss, wagging her short tail.

"What the—" Mike muttered from beneath the behemoth.

"Good dog," Kat said. "But it's time to get off. Off," she repeated, giving Lira the proper hand signal broad enough so she could see it.

The dog rose from Mike's chest and leapt off him, but not before accidentally kicking her hind leg into his stomach.

Mike didn't look good. He lay there, groaning and clutching his stomach.

Kat knelt by his side and stared at him anxiously. "Are you all right?"

He gave her a baleful look. "'Good dog'?"

"Well, yes," Kat defended herself. "It's important to praise the dog when she gets a cue right."

"So *you* sicced her on me?"

"No, but in her last film, she attacked the bad guy every time he walked in the door and tossed his keys on the table. You just happened to choose the same action. Come to think of it, you look a lot like him, too."

Still lying on the floor, Mike turned his head to one side and shot the dog a wary glance. Kat sighed in exasperation. Anyone could tell Lira wasn't dangerous—not when she wore such a goofy look of adoration on her fuzzy face.

"Great," he muttered. "I guess that explains why you yelled 'cut'."

"Of course. What did you think?"

Mike rolled his eyes. "I don't know. For all I knew, she came equipped with a switchblade."

"Don't be silly. Why would we want to hurt you?"

He sat up gingerly. "Maybe because of the way I treated you earlier today."

"Maybe," she said. It still hurt that he hadn't believed her.

Mike shot her the apprehensive look this time.

"Don't worry, I don't have any plans to hurt you . . . yet."

"I'm so relieved."

"Oh, come on." She extended a hand. "Stand up. Are you okay?"

He rose to his feet, disdaining her help, and rubbed the back of his head. "How do you think you'd feel if ninety pounds of hairy animal landed on you?"

"Probably not very good," she admitted. She felt the back of his head. "You've got a lump there where you hit the floor . . . and probably a hell of a headache."

He winced. "You got that right. Plus, I think she rearranged my internal organs on takeoff."

She remembered Mike's tendency to exaggerate the consequences of their little adventures. He hadn't changed. "Will you be all right?"

"I think I'll live," he said dryly and raked his hair out of his face.

"A-roo-rooo," Lira howled.

Mike jerked backward and stared at Lira. "What the—"

"It's the cue," Kat explained impatiently. "Remember, if you shove your fingers through your hair, she howls."

"Oh, yeah." He pierced her with a look. "Just how many of these cues does she have?"

"Quite a few—"

He stopped her with an upraised hand. "Never mind. Just tell me about the life-threatening ones."

Kat shrugged. "I've only been working with her for six months, so I don't know them all."

Mike groaned and eyed Lira as if he were afraid the lovable pooch was going to leap up and punch him or something.

"Don't worry," she assured him. "Most of them she'll only obey from her trainer. There are a few, though, she'll take from anyone. And, of course, Edward taught her to take some from me, too."

Now Mike was eyeing *her* with apprehension. "Like what?"

"Oh, mostly harmless. There's one—"

"No," he yelled when she raised her hand. "Don't *do* it, just tell me about it."

Mike had a point—he'd been on the receiving end of too many of Lira's cues already. "Well, if I splay my fingers outward and yell, 'stop,' she'll attack the person I'm pointing at. It's intended for my defense."

"Attack? Can you be more specific?" he asked, as if mentally preparing his defensive moves.

"So long as you're not harming me, she'll just take you down and sit on you. But if you try to struggle or hurt me, she'll attack your throat or . . . other vulnerable areas."

Mike gulped. "I see. Well, don't make that gesture, okay?"

She suppressed a smile. "You got it. Why don't you come into the living room and sit down?"

He gave her a peculiar look and muttered something that sounded like, "Thanks for inviting me into my own home." Then louder, "How'd you know I still lived here?"

She shrugged and followed him into the living room, Lira padding after them. "I didn't. I thought I'd find your parents and ask them to tell me where you lived."

"When Dad died, Mom moved to a condo in Florida and took only the minimum with her. She didn't want to stay here where everything reminded her of Dad, so I bought the house from her."

"I'm so sorry—I didn't know he'd passed." Why couldn't her mother tell her these important things?

"It's all right. You couldn't have known. He had a massive heart attack here at home." Changing the subject abruptly, he asked, "How'd you get in, anyway?"

"Oh, that was easy. The key was where your mother always left it—on the windowsill under the first pot."

Mike looked bemused. "I forgot it was there."

"Well, thank heavens I didn't, or Lira and I would've had to wait in the backyard."

He rubbed his stomach. "I might have preferred that."

Feeling a bit of remorse, she said, "Not when Joey has probably sicced the police on us. What if someone had seen her?"

Mike looked as though he wished he could turn her over to the police himself. Figuring discretion would be wise at this point, Kat gave Lira the cue to lie down. It was a little difficult to hide a dog of her size, but maybe if she were quiet, Mike wouldn't be so wary.

"You wouldn't want the police to find her, would you?" Kat asked.

He hesitated for a moment, evidently struggling with an internal conflict. "No," he admitted.

She took a deep breath, prepared to argue her case once more. She'd been practicing all afternoon. "Look, Mike—"

"Yes."

"No, wait. Let me finish—"

"Yes," he repeated more forcefully.

She stared at him in confusion. "Yes, what?"

"Yes, I'll help you."

Taken aback, all she could say was, "Why?" This was too easy.

"Because this time, you're right." Mike grinned at her with his funny familiar lopsided grin. She stared for a moment, entranced. She'd forgotten how much she missed his smile.

"I'm right?" she repeated, dumbfounded. Then, just in case he thought she doubted it, "Yes, of course I am. But how do you know that?"

"My receptionist overheard Joey talking about killing Lira for the insurance."

"You believed her and not me?"

He shot her an apprehensive look. "It wasn't like that."

That hurt. He'd always believed her before, followed her blindly on every whim, even when he was skeptical. And, she had to acknowledge, even when she was dead wrong.

"Come on, Kat," he pleaded. "You have to admit it didn't sound very plausible."

She decided to let him off the hook. "But you believe me now?"

"Yes. Let me make it up to you. I'll call the police and explain everything."

"You haven't called them already? Why not?"

He shrugged. "I didn't think about it. I was working . . . and trying too hard to find you."

"You were?" A warm feeling spread through her. He still cared.

"Yes, of course. Why didn't you answer your phone, or check your voicemail?"

She winced. "Because I . . . turned it off?" When he looked impatient, she added, "Joey was calling nonstop, so I stopped checking it. Sorry. Why did you want to find me?"

"I wanted to warn you that Joey has half convinced the police you've kidnapped her, and made them fear for their jobs if they don't find the famous Lira, Wonder Dog," Mike said sarcastically.

"Then we'd better not call them."

"How do you figure?"

"Even if they believe me, what do you think will happen to Lira if I give her back?"

"Nothing. They'll return her to her rightful owner and . . ." He paused. "I see the problem. You'd be right back where you started."

"That's right. And we'd give Joey a clear field to set up some sort of bogus accident. No, the best thing to do is find a safe place for Lira, somewhere we can hide her and they'll never find her."

A slow smile spread across his face. "I know just the place. Joey might find her there, but he'll never get away with hurting her."

Suddenly filled with hope, she asked, "Where?"

"Sanctuary. It's a shelter for animals, especially dogs. I do some pro bono work for them. They help abused and abandoned animals, so I'm sure they'll be willing to help a famous movie dog when her owner is ready to throw her away."

Kat raised an eyebrow at his sarcastic tone, but said only, "That sounds perfect."

"Good. I'll call them tomorrow and tell them you're coming."

"Whoa, wait a minute."

"What's wrong?"

"I'd rather you didn't call. I mean, I'd like to keep this a secret as long as possible. What they don't know, they can't tell . . . just in case Joey calls them."

He hesitated. "Sounds reasonable."

"And what's this about telling them I'm coming? Aren't you coming with me?"

He looked puzzled. "No, I have patients to see, commitments. But I'll tell you how to get there."

Disappointment filled her. "But, Mike, I was hoping you could help me with Lira. I'll have to keep her hidden and that's hard to do with a sheepdog this big—especially when I'm driving." She gazed up at him pleadingly. "Please, Mike? I really need you. Besides," she added, "you owe me."

"I owe you?"

"Yes," she said stubbornly. "For not believing me in the first place."

He glanced down at the dog and sighed. "Yeah, maybe I do. I'll have Aimee clear my calendar through the weekend, give my appointments to my partners." He gave her a rueful smile. "But you have to promise to pay my hospital bills when Lira does her quarterback sack again."

Joy filled her. "Oh, thank you, Mike." She threw her arms around him and gave him a big smacking kiss on the cheek.

Mike's arms came around her and she hugged him, thinking how good it felt to be with him again. It made her feel warm and fuzzy all over. Not wanting to analyze why it felt so good, she said, "Great. It's going to be just like old times."

Mike steeled himself against her appeal and peeled her arms away, saying flatly, "Yeah. Just like old times." Her exuberant hugs always made him feel on top of the world. But this was *not* going to be like old times. He might be getting involved in one of her crazy schemes again, but he wasn't going to let his heart get involved, too.

Detachment was called for here. And he'd gotten very good at detachment. That was, until Kat had come along and, in a few short minutes, managed to destroy what little control he had over his life.

Ignoring her confused expression, he said, "All right, let's eat dinner and make plans."

"Okay," Kat said cheerfully, looking like a bouncy puppy. She ordered Lira to stay, then followed him to the kitchen and peered into a few cabinets. "You haven't changed the house much," she observed. "Everything's still in the same place."

"Why should I change anything? I know where everything is."

She rolled her eyes at him. "Yeah, but isn't it a little boring?" She grabbed a can of soup and read the label. "Cream of mushroom. How exciting."

"I happen to like cream of mushroom soup."

She cocked her head and appraised him. "But haven't you ever wanted to go a little wild and try something totally different, like . . . cream of celery maybe, or—here's a wild idea—spicy Mexican tortilla?"

"I would if I thought I'd like them."

She shook her head. "You *are* a creature of habit. Here, let me help you." Instead of replacing the soup where she'd found it, she moved it two shelves down to sit by the boxed products. "There, isn't that better?"

"No," he said and moved the soup back to its proper place. "I'll never find it there."

"Nonsense." She moved it again. "Try to leave it there. Betcha can't."

"What? Of course I can. I just don't want to."

She leaned on the counter, propping her head on her

hand and grinning at him in amusement. "Uh-huh. Sure you can."

Annoyed, he snapped, "What are you saying?"

"I'm saying you're still a stick-in-the-mud."

"Because I like to be able to find things?"

"No, because you can't stand to have things out of place. You're a creature of habit."

"I am not." He glanced at the soup can and closed the door firmly. Bound and determined to prove her wrong, Mike was resigned to leaving the can out of place even if it nagged at him all night.

Kat's eyes sparkled with mischief as she chuckled. "Good for you. But I bet it's annoying as all get-out."

Maybe, but he wouldn't give her the satisfaction of thinking she was right. He changed the subject. "What would you like to eat?"

She shrugged. "What have you got?" She opened the refrigerator and freezer and gazed inside. "Good grief, you have enough food here to feed half of the city."

"And what's wrong with keeping a well-stocked kitchen?" he demanded.

"Nothing. I'm impressed. It's a lot better than mine."

"Let me guess," he said, turning the tables. "In the freezer, you have five different flavors of ice cream, all half-eaten, and a freezer-burned roast you bought on a whim but haven't a clue how to cook. In the refrigerator, there's a half-empty carton of milk, now curdled, some moldy cheese, a couple of boxes of leftover Chinese takeout, and five bottles of Perrier."

"Pretty close, but it's Evian, not Perrier, and only four flavors of ice cream." Her eyes twinkled at him. "You also forgot the cantaloupe."

This table-turning business hadn't worked out quite the

way he'd hoped. "Well, I like to be prepared, even if you don't. So, what do you want to eat?"

She continued grinning. "I'm tempted to ask for something outrageous, just to see if you have the proper fixings. But, anything's fine."

He didn't have anything defrosted so . . . "How about an omelet?"

"Sure."

Mike made dinner while Kat fed the dog. Was she right? Was he really a stick-in-the-mud? He thought about it for a while then berated himself. Look who was accusing him. Compared to pull-out-all-the-stops Kat, maybe he did appear a little stuffy. Who wouldn't?

No, he decided. He was normal. It was Kat who was off the deep end.

They planned their trip to Sanctuary over dinner, then washed the dishes and adjourned to the living room, taking their drinks with them. Lira wagged her tail in greeting but didn't move otherwise, keeping her nose between her paws. Apparently, she was worn out by the stress of attacking innocent veterinarians.

Kat glanced around, saying, "I like what you've done with this room."

"You do? It's not too *stuffy*?"

She sank down into his mother's favorite chair, which he'd upholstered to match the new beige and blue color scheme. Ignoring his sarcasm, she said, "No, I like the way you kept some of your folks' things and brought in a few new pieces and updated things. It looks homey. A little bland, maybe, but homey."

Mike sat on the couch and cocked an eyebrow at her. "Thanks. I think."

She smiled as she cuddled a throw pillow to her chest. "You're welcome. You know, this reminds me of all the good times we spent together. Doing homework upstairs, watching television here with Goldie lying by the fire, and eating your mom's terrific double fudge brownies."

He smiled at the memories. Kat had always insisted her dog Goldie belonged to both of them, and his mother hadn't objected to having the sweet-tempered golden retriever around. "Would you believe I have a half batch of those brownies on the counter?"

She laughed. "Of course you do." Her expression turned wistful. "I just wish I still lived next door. That would make everything perfect."

Not from his point of view. He'd finally managed to pry his heart from her oblivious clutches. Indulging in bouts of nostalgia about how much fun they'd had and how much he'd adored her was no way to keep it safe and whole.

He was over her, and he wanted to keep it that way. Starting now. "I have some reading to do, so let me show you to your room."

"The one that used to be your sister's?"

"No, I've converted that to a home office. You can sleep in my old room." Just where he'd longed for her to be throughout his adolescence. "The bed's made up and there are more linens in the hall closet if you need them."

"Okay," Kat said, though she appeared a bit disappointed that Mike wouldn't join her in reminiscing. "It's dark enough now. I'll just take Lira out and play with her for a while in the backyard . . . if that's okay with you."

"Sure."

He managed to avoid her for the rest of the evening and didn't emerge from his room until he heard her settle into bed. Firmly setting aside speculations of what she looked like between the sheets in his old room, he gave in to the impulse that had been nagging at him all evening. Quietly, he sneaked downstairs and put the soup back where it belonged.

CHAPTER FIVE

The next morning, Mike showered and dressed quietly so as not to wake Kat, then left her a note telling her he'd be home as soon as he changed his appointments, asking her to think of a way to disguise the famous dog.

It took a couple of hours to transfer his appointments to the other clinic veterinarians or reschedule them so he'd have Thursday through Sunday off, but Aimee gladly agreed to perform the extra work after he explained why he needed it.

Feeling pleased he'd be able to prove he *could* change his routine, Mike returned home in a good mood. Cheerfully, he opened the door and tossed his keys on the table.

He barely had time to think *uh-oh* before Lira hit him with a flying tackle. He went sprawling, and the dog had him helplessly spread-eagled on the floor once again, snarling at his exposed throat.

Somehow he found enough air in his lungs to gasp, "Cut" and make the appropriate gesture.

Thank heavens, it worked. Lira lumbered off him, looking pleased with herself and obviously expecting praise.

Kat came into the hallway and cocked her head, gazing down at him in amusement as he continued lying there, trying to regain his composure and the shreds of his dignity.

"Don't you dare say 'good dog,'" he warned.

Her smile widened. "You know, you really are a creature of habit."

Ignoring her, he sat up and ran a hand through his disheveled hair.

"A-roo-roooo," came Lira's immediate response.

Kat had the nerve to chuckle. "See?"

Groaning as he stood up, he said, "What? You couldn't kidnap a Chihuahua?"

He glared at her, then suddenly noticed the dog looked . . . different. The black half of her face had somehow become orange. He rose to his feet. "What happened to her?"

Kat shook her head in bemusement. "I tried to bleach her black spots white, but they turned orange instead."

"If this is your idea of a disguise, it leaves a lot to be desired."

"Hey, I tried. After this happened, I called a beauty shop. They said black hair always turns orange when you try to bleach it. How would I know that?"

How indeed. It didn't surprise him. "Well, it was a nice try," he admitted. "Did they tell you how to make it turn white?"

"Not really. I'd have to leave it in longer, but I already left the bleach on twice as long as they recommended. I guess dog hair is different than human hair. Besides, the hair-dresser said if I used any more, Lira's hair might fall out."

The doctor in him was forced to admit, "Not to mention what it might do to her skin."

"Right. And she's getting tired of spending time in the tub."

For the first time, he noticed that Kat looked a bit

disheveled, her hot pink pants and top soaking wet. His mouth quirked as he tried to hide a smile. "Looks like you had quite a struggle."

She grinned. "If you think I look bad, you should see your bathroom."

He groaned. "I think I'll pass."

Lira licked Kat's hand and she grinned. "See how sweet she is? She's apologizing."

"Yeah, but to the wrong person."

"Oh, come on, Mike. Lighten up."

Becoming a little annoyed at her constant references to his natural reserve, Mike changed the subject. Peering at the dog, he said, "She doesn't look all that different. In fact, she's more conspicuous than before. Isn't there anything you can do?"

"I can't think of anything—"

The phone interrupted her. "Hold on a minute," he said. "That might be the clinic."

He pulled out his cell. It was Aimee, distraught. "Calm down," he soothed, "and tell me what's wrong."

"It's that Joey Barton again," she whispered into the phone.

"Joey?" he repeated, and Kat moved next to him, gazing up at him anxiously.

"Yes, he can't find Miss Channing, so he somehow got the idea she's with you. He called to get your address. I think he's planning on coming over . . . with the police."

"Did you give it to him?"

"No, I told him I wasn't allowed to."

"Good for you."

"Yes, but he said he's going to call the police and have them get it from me," she whispered urgently.

"That's all right. We're leaving now, so even if he does get the address, he won't catch us."

"Good," Aimee said on a sigh of relief. "Don't let him hurt Lira."

"I won't," Mike promised. "And, Aimee? Thanks for calling. I owe you big time."

"Just make sure that dog's okay."

"I will."

He hung up and explained the situation to a wide-eyed Kat, concluding, "We need to get out of here. We don't have much time, but I'm afraid we won't be able to stop by your place to get anything. The police might be watching it."

"That's okay," she said. "I brought Lira's stuff and a few of my own things."

Mike nodded. "That just leaves me, then. I'll throw some clothes in a suitcase. Why don't you check out the kitchen and grab the brownies and some other things to munch on in case we don't have time to stop."

"Right."

He went upstairs to pack, then met Kat in the kitchen. "Which car shall we take?" he wondered out loud.

"Yours. Mine's a lime-green VW bug and Joey knows it too well. It's too conspicuous."

"Good point. Where is your car anyway?"

"Over on the next block—I didn't want them to connect my car with your house."

"Good thinking. I'll pull my car into the garage so we can pack without anyone seeing us—or Lira—then you can pull yours in when we leave."

After he packed, Kat met him at the garage door and stared at his minivan in disbelief. "Oh, no. You've turned into a soccer mom!"

"What?"

"You're not old enough to own a minivan," she stated, shaking her head.

"Don't be silly," he snapped. "I'm not a soccer mom—I'm a

vet, remember? The van comes in handy for transporting animals."

At the doubtful look on her face, he tossed the suitcase in the back and added, "What did you expect? A sports car?"

"Well, no, but couldn't you use something a little . . . peppier?"

"This suits me," he said flatly. "Now, do you want my help or not?"

"Yeah, I guess," she said in a doubtful tone. But after they finished loading the van and moved her car into the garage, she entered the van as if she feared she might turn into one of those dreaded soccer moms simply by sitting in the front seat.

Gritting his teeth, Mike started the van, but hesitated before taking off. Lira had her head on his shoulder and was gazing longingly at the window, her tongue lolling out and fogging up the window. "Could you tell her to lie down and stay there?"

"Why?" Kat asked. "With that orange fur, she doesn't look like Lira now."

"But she's very noticeable. What if Joey alerts the media that she's missing? People might remember seeing a sheepdog with half orange, half white face and put two and two together."

"He won't do that," Kat scoffed. "I mean, think about it. He doesn't want to draw any public attention to her being missing, especially since he plans on killing her."

"Humor me," Mike said. "I'm not used to having a dog's tongue in my ear while I'm driving."

"Okay, okay," Kat said and made a gesture he assumed was telling the dog to lie down.

The dog obeyed her signal, but looked up at him from the floorboard through her orange mop of hair, her bobbed tail wagging furiously.

Great. She and Kat thought this was nothing but an adventure. He shook his head and started the van.

Some adventure. Not only was Kat in trouble with the law, but she'd dragged him into it. Now they were both on the lam with a purloined pooch having a bad fur day.

He sighed. Just like old times.

CHAPTER SIX

KNOWING this was a really dumb idea, but finding himself doing it anyway, Mike eased out of the driveway and headed out of his Briargate neighborhood toward the freeway. Large, fluffy snowflakes drifted down to coat his windshield. Great—just what they needed.

"So, where is this Sanctuary, anyway?" Kat asked.

"Southwest of the Springs—in Dogwood, off Highway 115."

"Dogwood? I've never been there."

"You haven't? Well, you're in for a treat, then."

"Why do you say that?"

"They're as nutty about dogs as you are," he said with a smile.

"Is that why it's called Dogwood?"

"No, it's really named for the dogwood trees one of the founding families planted by the river, but they love dogs, and just about everything there revolves around dogs and other animals. Sanctuary is the official shelter, but really, the whole town is a shelter. You won't find any abused or neglected animals there except for those they rescue. The town won't tolerate it—they even have city ordinances to ensure the animals are taken care of."

Kat reached down to scrub Lira's ears. "Sounds like the perfect place for my girl, here."

Lira must have taken her affection as a sign that she could get up, because she rose back up to plaster her face against the window again. But since she did it on Kat's shoulder this time, Mike didn't object, not even when Kat rolled the window down a bit to give the dog some air.

"It is," Mike assured her. "They even have a local legend about a matchmaking dog."

She slanted him a skeptical look. "Really?"

"Really. The legend has it that back in World War II, a dog with a heart-shaped spot on his chest brought two soul mates together. They named him Match. Since then, there's always been a dog with a heart-shaped spot somewhere on its body that shows up when the previous Match passes, and they name them all Match."

"And they believe this?" she asked incredulously. "A dog who plays Cupid?"

He shrugged. "What's wrong with believing in romance?"

"Nothing—if you're prepared for disappointment when it doesn't last."

"They say it does, and have a lot of success stories to point to."

"Yeah, right. I know better. Romance is an illusion. After the romance fades, you have to learn to live with each others' foibles and annoying habits. Or not." She paused. "Mostly not."

Mike grimaced. "Sorry, I forgot about your parents." He'd seen how their constant bickering had upset Kat as a teenager. It was one of the reasons she'd spent so much time at his house with Goldie. "But not everyone's marriage turns out like theirs, you know."

"Fifty percent of all marriages fail. You really think Dogwood beats those odds?"

He shrugged. "I don't know. Haven't really researched it." But he hated seeing her cynicism. It was so unlike the normally bubbly and carefree Kat he remembered. She looked so sad, it touched something inside him.

"I always wondered . . . why did you come back to Colorado for college?" He'd hoped it was to be near him, but he knew that wasn't the case. "I figured you'd want to avoid the states where your parents lived."

She glanced down at her lap and fiddled with the buttons on her coat. "It was the only place I was really happy. You know—before things turned bad with Mom and Dad." She sighed heavily. "And then I ruined it with the Rat Incident."

"Kat, you didn't—"

She changed the subject abruptly. "It's snowing harder," she said as he turned onto I-25 South. "We'd better check the weather. Highway 115 isn't great with snow, is it? If I remember right, it's only a two-lane highway." She turned on the radio.

Mike sighed. He'd wanted to assure her that he'd forgiven her long ago. Didn't she know he'd forgive her anything? But apparently, she still felt guilty.

He turned his attention to the news. ". . . heavy snow expected tonight through tomorrow morning. In other news, Lira, the Old English sheepdog who is famous for so many blockbuster movies, has been filming her latest here in Colorado Springs. She has been kidnapped, and was last seen in Briargate in a green Volkswagen Beetle. Her owner has offered a generous reward for any information on her whereabouts. If you know anything, please call the station at—"

Kat switched off the radio abruptly, as if shutting off the announcer's voice would make the situation go away.

Mike frowned. "I thought you said Joey wouldn't alert the media."

"I didn't think he would," Kat said. "Why would he?"

Remembering what Aimee had said, Mike could think of one reason. "Maybe because now he can blame you if Lira shows up dead."

"Oh, crap. I never thought of that."

As usual, Kat hadn't thought it through at all.

She gave him a wide-eyed look. "What do we do now?"

"Maybe you should go to the police, explain everything. Aimee and I can back up your story. They're bound to understand, and it might ensure Joey won't kill Lira for the insurance money."

"No, I can't do that. What if they don't believe us? I'll be in jail and Lira will be dead. I can't let that happen."

"We'll both be in jail," Mike said grimly. "And I'll probably lose my license and my practice."

"Oh, no," Kat said, looking stricken. "I'm so sorry I involved you in all of this."

"So am I." But she was right about one thing—it was too late to turn back now. "I guess we'll have to see it through." Nervously, he shoved a hand through his hair, only to realize too late that was a really dumb thing to do.

"A-roo-rooo," Lira caroled happily out the open window.

Next to them on the freeway, the driver in a car full of teenagers rolled down his window. "Hey, that's Lira," one of them yelled. "Stop, you thief!"

Oh, crap. They honked and swerved toward him.

"Call 9-1-1," someone yelled.

"Get his license plate."

"Pull over, you filthy dognapper!"

Kat quickly shoved Lira down to the floorboard. "Lose them," she shouted.

He couldn't believe this was happening. Adrenaline

surged as Mike floored the accelerator and whipped in and out of traffic as best he could in the unwieldy van. Seeing a break in traffic, he zoomed across two lanes and careened off the freeway onto the Woodmen Road exit, to the indignant blaring of car horns.

"Hurry," Kat shouted.

"What do you think I'm doing?" he yelled. The roads were turning icy—this was a really bad idea.

"Not moving fast enough," she snapped back as she looked behind them. "They're three car-lengths behind."

Seeing his career flame out before his eyes, Mike took a right onto Woodmen Road and quickly blasted through the light as it was changing from amber to red. Seeing the other car was caught in traffic behind him, he took the second right turn, then made a series of random turns and got lost in a neighborhood. Finally, the adrenaline subsiding, he pulled into a cul-de-sac and tried to calm his breathing.

"That was quite some driving," Kat said admiringly. "You lost them."

Yeah, well, self-preservation was quite the motivator. And now that he'd been spotted driving the getaway van, he was definitely an accomplice.

"But for how long?" Mike snapped. "In case it escaped your attention, they got my license plate number. And this van isn't exactly inconspicuous."

"But it's white, like just about every other van I've ever seen."

A slight exaggeration. "Yeah, but this one has a sign on the side—with the name of my clinic on it!"

"Oh," Kat said softly. "That's bad."

He snorted. "Ya think?"

"So what do we do now?"

Mike thought furiously. "We ditch the van, get another car, and get a hotel room."

"Why get a room?"

"Because I don't want to have to make any more evasive maneuvers like that at night in icy road conditions."

Seeing Kat's panicked look, his anger dissipated. "Don't worry. We'll get Lira to safety and figure a way out of all this."

"You promise?" she asked, looking worried and adorable.

"I promise."

But how the hell was he going to pull that off?

CHAPTER SEVEN

KAT STARED INCREDULOUSLY at Mike as he pulled out his smartphone. "Now is not the time to check your email."

He shot her an exasperated glance. "I'm looking for a dog-friendly hotel nearby."

"Oh," she said in a small voice. Crap—she'd done it again. Gotten Mike in the middle of another one of her messes. "I'm sorry, Mike. I didn't—"

"Save it," he bit out. "Let's just concentrate on finding somewhere safe."

Kat nodded, feeling miserable. As Mike called to make a reservation, she rolled up the window to keep out the cold air and remove Lira's temptation to show her face.

"Okay," Mike said. "We have a room."

"*A* room?" Kat said in surprise.

"Yeah—with two queen beds. Don't worry. Your virtue is safe with me."

"I know that," Kat said lamely. He was the original boy scout. "I thought you meant it was for me only and you were going to leave me there."

He started the van and cautiously rolled out of the neighborhood. "When have I *ever* abandoned you?"

"You haven't. . . ." But there was always a first time.

She pulled out her phone and turned it on. Ten hang-ups from Joey and seven unheard voicemails, all from Edward. Plus one text: *You're fired!*

She didn't know why she was so surprised. What the heck had she expected when she kidnapped the most famous dog in the world?

He glanced at the phone. "Do they have your number?"

She nodded then looked up in sudden realization. "Do you think they can track me through the phone's GPS?"

"I don't know. Maybe."

Alarmed, she opened the window and tossed out the phone. It landed in the lane next to them where an SUV promptly ran over it.

"What the heck did you do that for?" Mike asked as she quickly rolled the window back up.

"I only get bad news on that thing. It was a good idea to get rid of it." And strangely liberating.

Mike shook his head and concentrated on driving, eschewing the highway and taking smaller streets until they reached the hotel. He parked at the far end of the lot, next to a bush.

"Why are you parking so far from the entrance?"

"The bush will obscure the sign on one the side of the van. And I'll find some mud or something to cover the other side and the license plate. With any luck, no one will spot it as the dognapping vehicle." He pulled gloves out of his pocket and put them on. "Stay here with Lira until I find out what room we're in. I'll try to get one on the ground floor with an outside door."

Lira whined from her position on the floorboard. "But Lira needs to go."

Mike lifted his hand, apparently to shove it through his hair again, but Kat grabbed it. "Not a good idea."

"Right." He glanced around. "The dog-walking area is right past the bush, but there's still a chance someone might recognize Lira."

"She still has to go. She's well-trained, but it's been awhile since she last went to the bathroom. You want her to go in the hotel room?"

"No, of course not. Hold on—I'm thinking." He snapped his fingers. "It's dark out, and the snow makes it harder to see. Let's disguise her."

"With what? You have sunglasses and a fake nose handy?"

He glared at her. "No, but Halloween was just last week. I dressed up for the kids at the clinic, and the costume is still in the back. If anyone asks, you can say you just came from a costume party or something."

He rummaged around in the back and came up with a wizard's cloak and pointed hat—both a bright purple with shiny gold stars. As he helped Kat get the dog's front legs into the sleeves, she said, "It's not exactly inconspicuous."

"No, but they'll notice the costume instead of the dog, and it'll obscure her shape."

"Oh. Yeah. Good idea." She fastened the hat with its elastic chin strap. Luckily, Lira didn't mind. She'd worn costumes before, in some of her previous movies. "Good girl," Kat said with a kiss to the sweet dog's head. "You're the consummate professional."

He glanced around. "Looks like the coast is clear. Go ahead. I'll use some of the mud here to cover the sign, then get our room."

Kat clipped on Lira's leash and took her to do her business, shivering in the cold. As Lira sniffed around for the perfect spot, Kat tried to keep her to the less well-lighted areas of the dog-walking area. Lira had a mind of her own, though, and kept pulling Kat to investigate more interesting smells.

Unfortunately, a man leading a dachshund appeared on the same errand.

"Come on," Kat muttered at Lira. "Do your thing. Quick, before he recognizes you."

As if she'd heard and understood, Lira finally squatted and did her business. Kat tried to hurry away, but the man shouted, "Hey you, stop!"

Oh, crap. All the blood drained from her face. Should she run or brazen it out and try to convince him this wasn't Lira? Running wasn't an option with the snow and ice on the ground. She put Lira half behind her to make her even less recognizable. "What?"

"Aren't you going to clean that up?" He pointed at the pile of poo Lira had left on the ground.

Oh. Whew. "Uh, I don't have anything to pick it up with."

"There's a dispenser and a trash can over there." He pointed and she realized it was in front of the bush they'd parked next to.

"Okay, thanks," she said, and quickly cleaned up Lira's mess before the guy could come any closer. Depositing the waste in the appropriate receptacle, she quickly crawled back into the van.

Mike joined her shortly, with a key in hand. "What's wrong? You look pale."

Kat shrugged. "I thought someone recognized Lira, but it was just a member of the Poop Police."

Mike shook his head. "I don't even want to know." He waved the key card at her. "We're in luck—the room is just a couple of doors down. Get your things and let's go."

With no one else around, they were able to get Lira into the room without incident.

After Kat wiped Lira's feet, the dog leapt up onto one of

the beds and lay there, staring at them. She looked ridiculous in the wizard costume, so Kat helped her take it off.

"I hope you're hungry," Mike said.

"I could eat."

"Good. After I checked in, I ordered us a pizza. Pepperoni with extra cheese, right?"

She nodded, touched that he'd remembered her favorite.

"There's a soda machine a few doors down. You want diet?"

She nodded again.

"Okay, I'll be right back."

Lira was probably hungry too. Glad she'd remembered to bring the dog's food, Kat scooped some out for her and placed it in the bowl. As Lira chowed down, Kat realized she'd forgotten to bring a water bowl. Glancing around, she spotted the ice bucket. Perfect. She filled it with water and placed it on the floor in the bathroom just as a knock came on the door.

She let Mike back in.

"Did you check the peephole to make sure it was me first?" he asked.

Uh, no. "I just assumed . . ."

"Well, don't assume. And if someone knocks again, take Lira and hide in the bathroom, okay?"

"Okay." Seeing Mike pacing the room, looking as if he would like to murder someone—preferably her—Kat added, "I'm sorry I got you into this. I didn't mean to—"

"'I didn't mean to,'" Mike parroted. "'It seemed like a good idea at the time.' Your favorite mantras. When are you going to learn to think before you leap?"

Couldn't he even take her sincere apology in the spirit it was offered? "Well, at least I'm not a boring stick-in-the-mud."

He turned to face her. "Are you talking about me?"

She shrugged. "Hey, if the stick fits, wear it up your butt." That's where it resided most of the time anyway.

He gaped at her. "Well, at least I'm not a flighty child who frolics through life not caring what happens to the people around her."

Is that what he really thought of her? Ouch. Kat shot back, "I care. I just don't let it define me. If you weren't Dr. Sheldon Cooper's clone, you'd know that."

He looked confused for a moment, then obviously made the connection with the *Big Bang Theory* character. "I am *not* like Sheldon."

"Yes, you are," she said, pleased to have rattled him.

"No, I'm not. I'm not a physicist, I don't have a roommate, and my interpersonal relationships are just fine."

"Yeah, right," Kat said with a snort.

"What does that mean?"

"Your OCD. I saw what you did with that soup can."

"I do *not* have OCD."

"People who have OCD don't know they have it."

"I don't even know how to respond to that."

"And," Kat added triumphantly, "like Sheldon, you're unfeeling and uncaring about other people."

"I am not," he protested. "I'll have you know my patients love me."

"The animals, maybe. But what about their owners?"

"Them, too. The problem is, I care too much. I just don't allow my feelings to erupt and spew all over everyone around me."

"Are you talking about me?"

"Who else?" He whirled, eyes blazing. "You know what we're really talking about here? It's your inability to commit, to act like a grown-up. You're so afraid of making a decision, so afraid of turning out like your parents, that you go too far in the opposite direction. You act impulsively. You know what that does? It makes you more like them, more uncaring of the people around you, more self-centered. You're so worried about your own personal freedom that you take away everyone else's freedom of choice by your foolhardy actions."

"Gee, tell me how you really feel," Kat said thickly.

Mike suddenly deflated and sat down on the other bed, shaking his head. "I'm sorry—"

"Oh, don't apologize," Kat said, waving her hands. "Sounds like this is the first time you've really told me the truth about how you feel." A small part of her wondered if he could be right, but she smashed that thought in a hurry.

He quirked a half smile at her. "No, not really. I—"

"I knew it," she exclaimed.

"What?"

"You still haven't forgiven me for the Rat Incident. It wasn't my fault—"

"Well, whose fault was it? It certainly wasn't mine. You let those rats out on purpose—"

"No, I didn't. It was an accident!" she blurted out.

He looked puzzled. "What? You said the school administration wouldn't treat them fairly, so you released them to freedom."

"I know that's what I said," she said mulishly.

"That's not what happened?"

She hadn't ever meant to tell him this, but she'd already blown it. Sighing, she said, "No. True, I did borrow your lab key and gathered all the rats in one big cage to make a point, and made demands. But I didn't let them out on purpose."

He appeared taken aback. "Really? What did happen?"

"When the big, burly security guard came barreling into the lab, he scared me and I . . . stumbled." She paused, embarrassed by her mistake.

"And?"

"And I accidentally fell against the cage latch. It opened, and the rats ran for it." At Mike's expression of disbelief, she added, "I tried to put them back in, but they were fast little suckers. The big, strong guard was apparently terrified of rats, so he panicked and I had to stop him from using his huge stomping feet on them."

Mike chuckled.

"It's not funny."

"Not that. Actually, I was thinking of what happened in the clinic earlier today. Apparently, Joey doesn't care for rodents either."

"Yeah, they creep him out."

"Well, our pet mouse got out, crawled up his pants leg, and he ended up dropping his pants to get rid of him."

Kat's mouth dropped open. "Don't tell me Joey went commando."

"No, worse—he was wearing SpongeBob SquarePants boxers."

She laughed. "Oh, wow. I wish I'd seen that."

Mike grinned. "Well, it entertained Aimee, the police officer, and a whole roomful of pet parents." He gave her a sober look. "So why did you lie and say you released the rats on purpose?"

She shrugged and plucked at a seam on the bedspread. "They were blaming you for loaning me the key."

"Well, I did do that, and knowing you, I should have known you had something crazy in mind."

She shook her head. "They thought you knew what I planned and wanted to kick us both out. I . . . I had to make sure they knew you weren't involved. So I told them I stole the key."

"So you lied to protect me? To make sure I didn't get kicked out of school?"

She shrugged. "No big deal. It was my fault anyway. But

this way, you didn't get in trouble for something I did." Kat wouldn't have been able to live with that.

"Why didn't you tell me?"

"Because I was embarrassed that I'd screwed up again. I didn't want to let you down. You're the best friend I ever had." She dropped her gaze, not wanting to see his reaction. Especially if he didn't feel the same way.

He settled on the bed next to her. "Thank you, Kat. That's the nicest thing anyone ever did for me. You were my best friend, too."

He gave her a one-armed hug, which seemed to break loose a whole dam of feeling she'd been holding back. She turned into his embrace and threw her arms around him. "I'm so sorry. Now I've done it again, and it's a whole lot worse."

He squeezed her tight, making her feel warm and comfortable and safe. "It's okay. We'll find a way through this. You'll see."

She didn't see how, but she nodded into his neck, not trusting herself to speak.

A knock came at the door. "That must be the pizza," Mike said.

She didn't want to leave his embrace—this was the best she'd felt in a long time. But she and Lira had to hide. She grabbed Lira's collar and led her into the bathroom and closed the door.

As she heard Mike talking with the delivery guy, she hugged Lira and vowed to ensure Mike wouldn't suffer for her mistake this time either.

CHAPTER EIGHT

As MIKE and Kat ate their pizza in relative silence, Mike didn't quite know what to say to her. They'd flung some awful accusations at each other, but after Kat's confession, he felt oddly touched by her sacrifice. Maybe she cared more than he realized. Of course, she'd called him the best "friend" she'd ever had—it didn't leave much opening for anything more, now, did it?

Suddenly, he no longer had an appetite, so he was glad when the phone rang. He checked the phone number. Aimee.

"Did you ever find your friend?" Aimee asked in concern.

"Yes—she showed up at my house." When Kat looked up in concern, he covered the microphone and told her reassuringly, "It's my receptionist. She's on your side."

"I'm so sorry," Aimee said. "The police were just here and they asked for your home address. I had to give it to them. You have to get out of there!"

"It's okay," he reassured her. "We're no longer there. We're at a hotel."

"A hotel?" she repeated. "Wow—you're a fast worker."

He grimaced. "It's not like that." He had to cut this off

right away. Aimee was a romantic, and since she wasn't having any luck finding a match of her own, she'd decided it was her mission in life to matchmake with the one doctor in the office who wasn't attached—Mike. He'd endured too many awkward blind dates with her fix-ups, and had finally made her promise to quit. It hadn't stopped her from championing potential life partners he met on his own, though. "Lira was spotted on the highway, so we had to find a place to hole up."

Kat crowded closer. "What's she saying?" she asked anxiously.

"Let me put you on speaker," he told Aimee. "So Kat can hear, too."

"Hi, there," Aimee said. "Are you and Lira okay?"

"We're fine," Kat said. "Mike is taking good care of us."

"I bet he is."

Kat appeared puzzled, but before Aimee could elaborate, Mike asked, "So, why are the police looking for me?"

"Since you admitted you two were 'old friends,' Joey insists you had also something to do with Lira's kidnapping."

Mike groaned. He so didn't need this. If the word got out he was involved in a dognapping case, his career could be over.

"I wouldn't worry too much," Aimee soothed. "They didn't seem too concerned, but Joey kept pushing it, saying the dog is in danger from Kat."

"She is not," Kat said indignantly. "Not from me."

"Well, I told them Mike wasn't able to get hold of you, and even if he did, there was no way a veterinarian was going to harm that dog. I also told them what I heard Joey say. I think they believed me, but they'll want to make sure."

"Good," Mike said in relief. "But someone spotted Lira in my van and I'm afraid they got my license plate number and saw the sign on the side of the van."

Aimee chuckled. "Oh, now I understand. I heard on the news that Lira was reported seen in a gray van. They gave a partial license plate, and said it appeared as if she'd been kidnapped by a veteran's organization."

He and Kat exchanged baffled looks. Kat said, "Well, the guys who spotted us were young and didn't seem very bright. The van does look gray with all the dirty snow on it."

That made sense. Mike nodded. "And with all the dodging and weaving I did, I'm sure they didn't get a good look at my plates."

Aimee added, "They probably just saw 'vet' and assumed veteran instead of veterinarian. After all, there are a lot of military in this town. Sounds like you're in the clear."

"Maybe with the media and the general public," Mike said. "But the police aren't that dumb. I'd like to find a different car, in case they're persuaded to treat this like a serious offense."

"How? By hotwiring a car in the parking lot?" Kat asked.

Kat's mind worked in mysterious ways. "Of course not. Adding a felony to the charges against us would make things worse. No, I'm talking about renting a car."

"But don't you have to give your name, credit card, and driver's license for that?" Aimee asked.

"Yes, but it's a risk we have to take if we're taking the dog to safety."

"No you don't," Aimee said. "You can borrow my car."

"And leave you with the van? No, I don't want to drag you into this and get you into trouble, too."

"What trouble? I'd just be loaning my boss my car at his request. What he does with that car is out of my hands." She paused. "Where are you taking Lira, anyway?"

Kat opened her mouth to reply, but Mike held up his hand to stop her. "Never mind that. What you don't know, you can't tell. And I can't leave you without a car." She only had the one.

"I'll figure something out," Aimee assured him.

"What if you borrow her car and rent her one instead?" Kat suggested. "If Aimee rents it in her name, it won't point back to you."

That was actually a good idea.

"Works for me," Aimee said.

"Okay," Mike said. "But I'm going to reimburse you for your expenses."

"I'll take it," Aimee exclaimed. "Want me to come right over? Where are you?"

"Not right now," Mike said. He peeked out the side of the blinds on the window. "It's snowing too hard, and the road conditions will be icy. Let's wait until the morning and see what the roads are like."

"Okay," Aimee said, sounding disappointed. "What time?"

He thought for a moment. "Not too early—give the snow plows time to clear the roads. Let me do some research, see what time the car rental agencies open, and I'll text you with a time."

"How about breakfast?" Kat asked.

"The hotel offers a free breakfast with the room," he told her.

"Yeah, but I'm not so sure it's a good idea for me to be seen in public."

Good point.

"No problem," Aimee said cheerily. "I'll bring you breakfast. Mike can pay for it. What would you like to eat?"

As Kat and Aimee discussed tomorrow morning's meal, and Kat gave her the hotel name and room number, Mike thought quickly. Kat was right about potentially being recognized. He'd do something about that tomorrow morning as well. When they were done, Mike hung up.

"Wow," Kat said. "You have a great employee there."

Mike nodded, and decided not to warn her of Aimee's penchant for playing Cupid. Instead, he said, "She's the best."

"No," Kat said. "You are. And I can't keep letting you pay for everything. This is my problem, not yours."

"Don't worry. I can afford it. Besides, you don't want a credit card trail in your name, in case the police do get serious about this."

"Well, I'm going to pay you back for every penny you spend on us," Kat said stubbornly. "After I find a new job. Edward—Joey's uncle—fired me by text."

Okay, now her tossing the phone out the window made more sense. Kat did have a habit of jettisoning anything in her life she found distasteful. He shrugged. It wasn't as if he was going to bill her. He'd joined her voluntarily in this madness.

"And if I don't go to jail," she muttered.

He moved toward her, intending to offer comfort, but Lira, evidently sensing Kat's distress, nosed Kat and looked up at her as if to ask her what was wrong. Kat enveloped the big dog in a hug and buried her face in Lira's fur. "No matter what," she said, her voice thick, "I'll make sure they don't hurt you."

Damn. He hated to see her cry. "We both will," Mike assured her. "And I'll do my best to make sure both of you are safe and jail-free." He had no idea how he was going to do that, but there was something about Kat that had always made him want to play Sir Galahad and ride to her rescue. Even if the maiden in distress didn't want or need him to.

They spent the rest of the evening watching the old movies Kat loved, including *The Trouble With Angels* starring Hayley Mills. Mike couldn't help but draw similarities between her character's "scathingly brilliant" ideas and Kat. Silently, of course. He didn't want to fight any more.

They made an early night of it, Mike taking one bed and Kat and Lira sharing the other. As Mike tried to sleep, he couldn't help but hear Kat cuddling with Lira in the next bed. Damn, if he wasn't jealous of a big hairy dog.

KAT WAS ENJOYING a blissful dream of frolicking in a meadow with Lira and Mike when a nudge at her shoulder woke her up. "Wha—?" she muttered.

The nudge came again, more urgently. Lira. Kat peered at the bedside clock. Five thirty-two? "Can't you wait?" Kat complained.

Mike came out of the bathroom. She should have known he was an early riser. "What's wrong?" he asked.

"Lira needs to go outside."

"Oh." He paused for a moment, then said, "I'll take her, so no one sees you. I'm dressed already anyway."

"No, it's okay. She's my responsibility. I'll do it." She moaned as she rolled out of bed, still wearing the clothes she'd worn yesterday. "I doubt there'll be many people out at this time of the morning anyway. Let me just use the bathroom first."

Kat used the bathroom, brushed the fuzzies from her teeth, then bundled up against the cold. Mike was already dressed to go outside and was putting the wizard costume on Lira again. "I told you I'd do it," she said. He'd done enough for them already.

"You're not a morning person, I see."

She glared at him, and he had the gall to chuckle. "I should have known you are," she said, feeling annoyed for no reason she could fathom.

"I thought I'd run interference, check it out first to make sure no one is around before you take Lira out."

Kat grumbled, but had to admit privately that it was a good idea as she tugged a knit hat down around her ears and tucked her hair inside.

"Wait here," Mike said. "I'll let you know when the coast is clear."

Once Mike gave her the all-clear, Kat took Lira out to the dogwalking area. Her breath escaped in a white cloud and her cheeks and nose hurt from the cold. She crunched through the new snowfall—about six inches now—and clutched her arms around her chest in an attempt to get warm. Good thing she hadn't tried to go on the lam in her little VW. Then again, Mike's van wasn't much better in the snow. With any luck, it would warm up today and melt the ice from the roads.

Lira finally found a suitable location to do her business without being spotted. Kat cleaned up after her so they wouldn't be hounded by the Poop Police again, and let Lira back into the room.

"Wait," Mike said when Kat started to follow her inside. "We should probably get what we need out of the van before Aimee arrives and other people head out for breakfast."

"Good idea." Last night, they'd brought in only what they thought they'd need for the night.

They grabbed the rest of the supplies as well as the duffel bag of Lira's treats and toys. As Mike closed and locked the van, Kat spotted someone coming their way. Oh, crap. That someone was in a uniform.

"Police," she hissed, then frantically tried to figure a way to cover the sign on the side of the van. Mike's efforts last night had only partially obscured it.

Before Mike could look around, she plastered her back-side against the sign and grabbed Mike's coat lapels, pulling him in close. "Kiss me," she muttered.

Mike's eyes widened, then his mouth quirked in a devilish

smile—a sexy, to-die-for expression as he leaned in to do her bidding.

His mouth covered hers, and she forgot all about the cold metal against her backside as Mike pressed his warm body against her and his lips moved against hers. She'd only intended to pretend they were newlyweds, but Mike was evidently of the method acting, immerse-yourself-in-the-role kind of guys.

Not that she objected. He poured his entire being into this one kiss, as if she was the only girl in the world, and he was the only guy. *Oh, my.* She lost herself in the heady sensations he engendered, drowning in his warmth and seduction, wishing it would never end.

"Excuse me?"

Damn. Who was bothering them?

The voice came again. "Uh, excuse me, folks?"

Oh, the cop. Feeling as though she were drugged—now there's a drug she wouldn't mind getting addicted to—she pulled slowly away from Mike and peeked over his shoulder at the cop, ensuring only her eyes were visible.

"I'm so sorry, officer," she drawled in her best imitation of a Southern belle. "But this is our honeymoon, and I'm afraid I just can't resist this big old strong man of mine."

Mike twisted to regard the policeman, keeping his body between her and the cop. "I'm sorry. We'll take it inside."

"No matter," the policeman said. "I was just wondering if you've seen a large dog around here. A sheepdog."

Panicked. "No—" Kat started to say, but Mike cut her off.

"I did see a dog like that," Mike said. "It was before you came out to join me, honey," Mike told Kat, his eyes telling her to keep her mouth shut. "A woman put the dog in a light-colored van and drove away."

Wow, Kat thought admiringly. That was a much better lie

than hers. Mike was good at this. She decided to let him handle it.

"How long ago was that?" the policeman asked.

Mike shrugged. "About half an hour ago?"

"Did you happen to notice what they looked like or where they were headed?"

Mike shook his head. "Sorry, I was ... distracted."

He gazed down at Kat tenderly, making it obvious where his thoughts had been. To the cop, anyway. Kat knew better, but damn if she didn't wish it was real. She beamed back at him lovingly, hoping the cop bought it.

"Thank you for your time, sir," the cop said politely. "Though you might want to take that inside before you get frostbite on some important extremities," he added with a smile.

"Yes, sir," Mike said. And, after one last kiss, he added, "Let's go inside and get warm, honey."

Oh, yeah. Too bad he was just pretending. But she giggled for the cop's benefit and picked up the duffel bag of toys as they strolled slowly back to their room, their arms around each others' waists. Mike steered her gently to put her back against the door of their room, and leaned down as if to give her another one of his devastating kisses. "Is he gone?" he asked as he nuzzled her neck. "I don't want to open the door and chance him spotting Lira."

"Al—almost," Kat said. Okay, so she lied. She didn't see the cop anywhere in sight, but she didn't want Mike to stop. Oh, she knew it wasn't real, but she really wanted it to be. Who knew the staid, stick-in-the-mud vet would be such a wonderful kisser?

Mike glanced toward where the cop had been. "I don't see him."

"He, uh, just turned the corner," Kat lied.

For a moment, Mike didn't move. But he was shaking.

Was he laughing silently at her? Really? "We can go in now," she said reluctantly.

Mike nodded, then with a wide grin, he pulled all his delicious warmth away from her and slid the key card from his pocket.

He gestured her inside with a smoldering look and she went, feeling her face flame hot. "Wow. It's warm in here." She fanned herself and pulled off her coat and hat.

His smile widened.

She turned away, not knowing what to do with herself. "I think I'll, uh, take a bath." She grabbed her suitcase and headed for the bathroom, tossing over her shoulder, "Great acting, Mike. Really. I think you deserve an Oscar for that performance."

As she closed the bathroom door and slumped against it in relief, Kat thought she heard him say, "Acting? Who was acting?"

Her heart leapt, but she sternly told it to stay still. She must have misheard it. After all she'd put him through, Mike couldn't possibly be interested in her.

Could he?

CHAPTER NINE

"WELL, THAT WAS INTERESTING," Mike murmured. Of course, she'd kissed him only to avoid the policeman, but her reaction to the kiss was fascinating, to say the least. Awesome, delectable, the kiss had satisfied the one desire he'd had ever since he met her, and ignited another.

In high school and college, her friendship had been far more important than a fleeting kiss, so he'd never even made the attempt. She obviously hadn't felt the same way about him, so he'd figured it was a no-go. He wasn't her type—at least, not the type she went for back then.

Strange how she always seemed to attract guys who were as commitment-phobic as she was, one after the other. It had killed him when they inevitably dumped her and he had to pick up the pieces of Kat's broken heart. Well, her lacerated pride anyway. She hadn't really let anyone get close enough to let them affect her heart.

With a sudden burst of understanding, he realized she'd done it deliberately, whether consciously or not. She went for the ones who were bound not to stick around, so she wouldn't get her heart engaged, so she'd never get hurt or end up in the same situation as her parents.

If history was any indication, she was still doing the same thing now. That meant she wouldn't know what to do with a guy like him, one who actually cared about her. A smile stretched his lips. No problem—he'd enjoy showing her.

And, though he'd felt like she had forced him into another madcap situation, he was starting to feel more in control of it, more like himself.

A sudden clatter drew his attention. Lira had nosed the apparently empty ice bucket. Mike refilled it with water and fed her, then pulled out his phone to text Aimee with some requests. Forty-five minutes later, Mike realized Kat was still in the bathtub. She must be a prune by now. Did she always take so long?

No, he realized with amusement. No doubt she was delaying the time when she had to face him again. She was probably trying to figure out how to react, what to say to him. He wondered idly what she'd come up with.

Lira nudged him with one of her toys, and he played tug with her, asking, "What do you think, girl? How will she react? Let's see . . . it could go one of three ways." He tossed the knotted rope onto the bed and Lira leapt up to retrieve it, then brought it back for more tug. "Number one, she could be breezy and offhand like the kiss was no big deal. Number two, she could ignore it and pretend it never happened, or number three, she could get serious and want to discuss what happened and what it means to both of us."

Lira snorted, and Mike grinned. "Yeah, number three isn't an option, is it? I'm betting on number two."

The bathroom door opened then, and Lira bounded over to greet Kat, who emerged vigorously toweling her tousled curls. The better to obscure her face, he was sure.

"Who are you talking to?" Kat asked.

"Just Lira," he said.

"Oh." She continued to rub the towel on her head and avoided looking at him. "Oh, by the way, sorry about attacking you out there. You know it was just to avoid the cop, right?"

Hmm, breezy and offhand—she'd surprised him by going with number one. Mike chuckled. "I figured you'd seen so many old movies where this happened that you panicked and it was the first thing that popped into your head—one of your 'scathingly brilliant' ideas. You went with your impulses, as usual."

"Yeah." She gave him a strange look as if she weren't quite sure how he was taking this. "Uh, you know, I didn't get much sleep last night. I think I'll take a nap until your friend gets here."

Way to avoid the subject. Classic Kat. Mike nodded and opened the door to the outside.

"Where are you going?" she asked in surprise.

"Nowhere. I'm just putting the Do Not Disturb sign on the door handle."

"Why?" she asked, looking alarmed.

"So the maid doesn't come in to change our beds and see Lira," Mike explained, suiting action to words and closing the door behind him. But he couldn't resist adding, "Besides, I think I'll join you."

Kat's face flashed red. "J-join me?"

He couldn't quite read the expression on her face, but he wished he was a mind reader so he could know what was going on in that quirky brain of hers.

"In taking a nap," he clarified. Then, when she didn't look any less panicked, he relented. "On the other bed."

"Oh."

She looked simultaneously relieved and disappointed, though she tried to hide her expression by leaning over to pet the dog. He couldn't resist teasing her a little. "What did you think I meant?" Maybe it was evil of him, but he did enjoy seeing her squirm.

"That's what I thought you meant," she said hurriedly.

Riiiiight.

She kept her attention on Lira. "Come on. Let's get you some water and something to eat."

"I did that already," Mike told her.

Kat hesitated. "Ah, okay. Thanks. Then it's naptime, sweetie. Come on, up on the bed."

Lira joined Kat on one bed while Mike lay on the other, his hands behind his head. He tried not to think about Kat lying in the next bed, and her response to their kiss. Suddenly, this adventure didn't seem so bad.

He didn't know about Kat, but he sure wasn't able to get any rest—not with his mind reliving that kiss over and over, and fantasizing about doing it again. So he was relieved when a knock finally came at the door.

With the speed at which Kat leapt up and hustled Lira into the bathroom, it didn't appear as if she had slept either.

He waited until she and the dog were safely in the bathroom, then opened the door. As he expected, it was Aimee, juggling a large shopping bag, a bakery bag, and a cardboard drink takeout container.

He relieved her of some of her burden and gestured her inside. "It's okay," he called to Kat after he closed the door. "It's Aimee."

Kat came out of the bathroom, and Lira bounded over to greet their guest. As Aimee petted the friendly dog, Kat said, "Thank you so much for helping us." Her eyes lit on the bakery bag. "And bringing breakfast!"

"No problem," Aimee said with a laugh. "I was glad to do it." She turned to Mike. "By the way, I told the other partners and office staff that you have a family emergency, in case the police ask why you're gone. I brought what you asked for." She nodded at the shopping bag.

She handed him his coffee—just the way he liked it—and gave Kat what smelled like hot chocolate. "I bought assorted pastries, not knowing what you'd like," she told Kat.

Kat rummaged in the bag. "Bear claws—yum." She pulled one from the bag and Mike looked inside. Just as he suspected, Aimee had brought his favorite—apple fritters.

"Thank you," Mike said. "Efficient as always."

Aimee beamed at him, and Mike marveled once again that she had trouble finding someone of her own. The brunette was young, pretty, confident, and competent. So maybe she carried a few extra pounds—what man didn't like curves?

They spent a few minutes satisfying their hunger, then Kat asked, "What's in the other bag?"

"Some things Mike asked me to pick up," Aimee said, drawing the bag closer. "First off, I got some large piddle pads from the clinic." She pulled them out and handed them to Kat. "Will Lira use them?"

Kat nodded. "She doesn't like them, but she'll use them." She gave Mike a surprised look. "Good idea—I wasn't looking forward to taking her out in the bright sunshine, even in her wizard disguise."

She told Aimee about the disguise, and Aimee laughed, then said, "Speaking of disguises, Mike asked me to bring something else." She reached into the bag and a small box fell out—a Trojan Pleasure Pack.

Alarm flared in Mike, especially when he saw Kat's shocked expression. "I did *not* ask her to bring those," he told her vehemently. What the hell was Aimee thinking?

"Oops," Aimee said with a giggle. "That was my idea. And it wouldn't disguise anything now, would it?"

"I wouldn't know," Kat said with a small smile as her gaze strayed to his lap.

I'm sooo glad she's amused by this. Mike resisted the urge to cross his legs. Lord save him from matchmaking assistants.

"This is the disguise I meant," Aimee said. She pulled out a package of hair dye and handed it to Kat.

"You want me to dye my hair black?" she asked, looking alarmed.

"No," Mike said, glad for the change of subject. "That's for Lira. Instead of bleaching the black parts of her hair, I thought it would be better to make her look black all over."

"It's not permanent," Aimee assured her. "And I didn't know how many boxes she'd need, so I bought several. Plus I brought some old towels so you won't ruin the ones here."

"Oh, yeah," Kat said. "Good idea."

"I brought some clippers, too," Aimee said. "In case you want to clip her like a poodle and make her look totally different."

Kat looked hesitant. "Maybe not. If she's able to resume her film schedule, it would take too long for her hair to grow out again."

Mike exchanged a concerned glance with Aimee, then looked at Kat. "Do you really think everything will go back to normal?" he asked gently. Kat had to face facts, and he wasn't sure she totally understood the seriousness of what she'd done.

"Maybe not," Kat said, not meeting his eyes. "But at least this way, we have the option."

Mike let it go, not wanting to call her on it in front of Aimee.

"Okay," Aimee said. "Then this might help. I brought some ribbons to put her hair in a froufrou topknot. You know, like they do with Maltese, Shih-Tzu, and other dogs whose hair flops in their eyes. That should help with the disguise, too."

Kat smiled at her. "Yes, it will. Thanks."

Aimee beamed. "In case you wanted to try it, I also brought a wig for you that I used this year for Halloween—it's black, cut in a severe bob." She glanced at Kat's blond, curly hair. "Nothing like yours." Not like Aimee's either, who wore her dark brown hair in a long wavy style.

Kat grinned. "You're good at this."

Aimee waved that away. "Not really. This was all Mike's idea. He also said you hadn't brought many clothes, so I picked some up for you. The only thing open was Walmart, so it's not exactly high-end stuff, but at least you won't have to wear the same clothes for days."

She pulled out some pants and tops, and Kat checked the labels. "How did you know my size?"

Mike gestured at her overnight bag. "I checked in there."

Kat's face turned red again. "You looked through my underwear?"

Yes, and it had been a revelation. Who knew the tomboy he'd grown up with had developed a passion for sexy lingerie?

"I told him to," Aimee told her. "I had to know what size to get. He said you were taking a bath." She waggled her eyebrows suggestively at Kat.

Stop that, Mike wanted to say. *Don't scare her away.*

"Yes, I was. Alone," Kat said with a stern look.

Whew. Apparently, she had Aimee's number.

Aimee added," Don't worry—I got stretchy pants and flowy tops and sweaters, just in case I'm off."

Kat looked doubtfully at the "flowy" blouses and Mike hid a grin. They were more Aimee's style than hers—Kat preferred T-shirts or casual wear, and these were decidedly feminine. But it would be good for her to try something new, something to go along with her sexy lingerie. And he couldn't wait to see her in one of those.

Since they'd all finished eating by now, Mike stood and took charge. "While Aimee and I rent a car for her, why don't you change Lira's hair color, then change into some clean clothes?"

Kat stared at him, stunned and apparently unable to argue with his priorities. "Aye, aye, sir. Any other orders, sir?"

"No, that should do it." He slipped on his coat and gloves and smiled. As he went out the door, he grinned. It was good to feel in control again.

CHAPTER TEN

THOUGH THE DOG WAS WELL-BEHAVED, coloring Lira's hair was much harder than Kat expected. There was so much of it, and it was hard to keep the dog from shaking the dye everywhere. Thank goodness Aimee had brought several bottles. She'd needed them all. And without the extra towels Aimee brought, the hotel's linens would have been an utter disaster. Kat's clothes already were.

Aimee was one special lady—smart, efficient, pretty, and a lot of fun. Why had she and Mike never gotten together? They had a lot in common and seemed perfect for each other. "Maybe it's because she works for him," Kat said to Lira as she toweled the dog's wet hair vigorously. That would go against Mike's Boy Scout attitude.

But she hadn't seen even a speck of interest from either of them in each other, and she'd looked. Maybe the old adage about opposites attracting was true. If so, Kat and Mike would be a shoo-in.

No. Don't go there. Kat's face grew warm as she thought about how she'd thrown herself at him earlier and she squirmed with embarrassment. What had she been *thinking?* Obviously, she hadn't been thinking at all, as usual.

She was left with the contradictory desires of wanting to do it again . . . and running as fast as she could in the other direction.

For a moment, she allowed herself to wonder what it would be like to kiss him again, to indulge her senses in the admirable man he'd become. Maybe even have a real relationship.

Nope. Bad idea.

She'd paused in her toweling of Lira to daydream, and now the dog licked her face, as if asking *why not?* After all, he seemed to want to explore this strange attraction as much as she did, so why shouldn't she?

The answer was obvious. He was the only person she'd ever had in her life who had stuck by her through everything —through her parents' divorce, her crazy relationships with other men, and even the Rat Incident. If she were honest, she hadn't left Colorado because he was angry with her—she'd left because she felt so guilty about involving him in one of her messes.

And now that he was back in her life, she didn't want to lose the best friend she'd ever had. Kissing and . . . and anything else would just complicate things. She was bound to do something to screw it up, and lose his friendship forever. Best not to go there.

Lira moved restlessly, and Kat decided to give the dog a break. She'd been very good, and Kat had gotten the worst of the water out of her fur. Lira was just damp now. Kat removed the towel, and Lira gave a vigorous head-to-tail shake that sprayed the remaining droplets around the bathroom, then made a break for it and ran to the bed to roll around on the bedspread. Luckily, Mike had placed an old blanket from his van there for her.

While Lira reveled in her freedom, Kat took a look around the bathroom. She'd confined most of the mess to the tub and its surround, but if she didn't clean it up right away, the little specks and splotches of dye might become more permanent. She used the old towels Aimee had brought to mop the floors and walls—sheesh, even the ceiling—then dropped the soggy towels in the huge shopping bag Aimee had brought. First chance she had, she'd take them to the dumpster. No sense in keeping them—or in leaving evidence behind.

Just as she finished, she heard someone at the door. Concerned that it might be the maid, she rushed out of the bathroom to grab Lira. The door opened and she heard Mike call, "It's just me. I got us some—"

He cut off when he caught a glimpse of her disheveled state. Realizing she must look like a drowned rat, Kat said, "Sorry, I've been wrestling a wet dog. She gave me a bath, too."

Mike nodded slowly as his gaze drifted down to her chest. She glanced down. Oh, crap. She looked like a contestant in a wet T-shirt contest. And her sheer bra sure didn't hide much.

Feeling awkward and knowing her face must be as red as fire, she crossed her arms over her chest. "Good idea, dying her all black. It looks a lot better than that orange mess." She nodded toward the bed where Lira squirmed on her back, as if trying to scratch an impossible itch.

Mike's gaze moved from Kat's crossed arms to the bed. "Good job," he said. "She doesn't really look like an Old English sheepdog any more. More like a Bouvier. If anyone asks, we can tell them she's a Bouvier mix."

Kat nodded, still keeping her arms crossed. "And with the blue hair ribbons Aimee brought, we can pretend she's a male dog. After all, it's not like anyone's going to check." And the fur back there would be enough to hide the evidence of her real gender.

Mike's gaze returned inexorably to her, and Kat felt uncomfortable. She couldn't keep standing there with her arms crossed over her chest, so she said, "I'm a mess after dying Lira's hair. I need to, uh, change into some dry clothes."

He nodded wordlessly again, and Kat grabbed the clothes Aimee had brought for her and practically ran into the bathroom.

As she leaned against the closed door and closed her eyes in embarrassment, she berated herself for being an idiot. Then, when she opened her eyes and saw her reflection in the mirror, she was even more stunned. Good Lord, it looked like she'd stripped naked and paraded in front of him. *Gack!* He didn't think she'd done this on purpose, did he?

Please, no.

Hot embarrassment filled her as she dropped her wet— and now ruined—T-shirt on the floor and stripped off the rest of her clothes. She toweled herself vigorously then got dressed in the clothes Aimee had bought her. Those flowy tops were out of the question—she didn't want to look like she was trying to seduce Mike. She pulled on knit pants and a vee-necked sweater instead and glanced in the mirror.

Well, crap. They clung to her modest curves and made her look a lot more feminine than she preferred. But it was either this, change back into the wet clothes, or go naked.

Sighing, she added her ruined clothes to the bag of wet towels, then steeled her spine and went back out in the room. Mike had set out some deli sandwiches, chips, and sodas. "Is that what took you so long?" Kat asked.

He glanced up at her and his gaze lingered on her curves. Though his smile showed that he liked what he saw, thank goodness he didn't say anything. She resisted the urge to cross her arms and cover the areas he'd already seen too much of.

"Yes—I wanted to get some things to tide us over until tomorrow morning and I extended the hotel room another night. We won't be going anywhere tonight."

"We won't?"

"Have you looked outside recently?"

"No, I was too busy dying Lira's hair." She went to the window and peeked outside. Giant snowflakes floated to the ground, joining the ones already there. "Oh, wow. There must be eight inches out there already."

Mike nodded. "And more expected this afternoon and evening. I rented Aimee an SUV so she could get home okay, but though her car has all-wheel drive, I don't want to chance it on the ice all the way to Dogwood. She'll arrange to have someone pick up the van when the roads are better."

Worried, Kat asked, "But shouldn't we get Lira to safety right away?"

"She's safe enough here," Mike reminded her. "No one knows we're here." He gestured at the food on the table. "Come, eat."

Kat sighed and joined him. The room only had one chair next to the small table, so he sat on the bed and gave her the chair.

"Looks good," she said, selecting a turkey sandwich. "Thanks for thinking of this."

"No problem. I also got Lira a water bowl so she doesn't have to use the ice bucket." He smiled. "She seems to like it."

Sure enough, the dog was slurping up water like she was dehydrated or something. Lira's appearance gave her a start. She looked so odd, all black like that, not at all herself. And if Kat didn't recognize her, maybe no one else would either.

"So, have you thought through what you want to do once we get Lira to Sanctuary?" Mike asked.

"No, I haven't thought that far ahead." And, knowing that was the answer he'd expected, she added defensively, "I was too busy saving her life."

"I understand, but you might want to think about it now. Sanctuary rescues animals and provides immediate shelter for those who have been abused, mistreated, or abandoned, but their primary mission is to find loving homes for all of them."

"Oh," Kat said in a small voice. "I thought they'd take care of her for the rest of her life."

"I don't think that's possible," Mike said gently. "They rely on donations to keep the dogs in food and shelter, but they're all in cages. Comfortable cages with beds, blankets, and toys, but cages nonetheless." He paused, then asked softly, "Is that what you want for Lira?"

"No," she admitted. "Then why did you suggest Sanctuary in the first place?"

"I suggested it only as a temporary measure. Once Lira is in their facility, they won't release her to anyone unless they've been fully vetted and approved to provide a good home."

"Not even to her owner?"

"Not even then. I told you the city ordinances in Dogwood all weigh heavily in favor of the animals. Joey won't be able to get hold of her unless they're satisfied she'll be safe with him." He chewed a bite thoughtfully, then said, "He seems to be the kind of guy who goes off half-cocked. Do you think his uncle really meant for him to kill Lira?"

She'd wondered about that herself. "Maybe. I don't know."

"Maybe you could call his uncle, feel him out? If he didn't mean for Joey to do away with Lira, Edward can call him off. And, if he did mean it, well . . . knowing that you're onto him might prevent him from trying to collect the insurance on her, especially if you hint that you'll tell the insurance company his plans."

"How will that help?"

"I doubt they'd pay out if they think he deliberately killed the dog, and if there's no monetary gain, there's no reason for him to do anything to her. Why don't you talk to him?"

Kat sighed. If only it were that easy. "I would, but I had his cell number on my phone." Which was now lying smashed in some odd neighborhood. "I didn't memorize it."

"Well, maybe if you called the set . . ."

She shook her head. "He's out of town for a few days, and won't be there. I really doubt they'll give me his cell number now." Before he could say anything, she added, "And they won't give it out to you, a stranger."

"Have you thought about adopting her yourself?"

Kat glanced at the lovable dog. "I'd love to, but I don't have a job anymore, and I don't even have a place to live—I was staying in the movie set trailer for the duration of the film." She hadn't thought far enough ahead to know what she was going to do after the shooting ended.

Shooting . . . She grimaced. Bad choice of words.

"You can stay with me until you find a new job," Mike said diffidently. "I have plenty of room."

Kat blinked back sudden tears. "Thank you, Mike." It was good to know she had somewhere to go, but she was determined to *not* need his help. "So what are we going to do until tomorrow morning?" Not that she was suggesting anything. Really.

"I can think of a few things," he said with a smile.

"What?" she asked warily, afraid he'd think she was coming on to him.

"Remember when we had snow days when we were kids?"

She nodded, smiling at the memory. "We binge-watched

your mom's collection of old movies and TV shows." They'd lie on the floor together, munching popcorn, drinking hot chocolate, and watching movies. "But it's not like you brought those with you, did you?"

"The next best thing—I have my tablet and a Netflix subscription."

"Perfect," she said with relief.

"I even have a bag of popcorn and some hot chocolate to heat up for later."

How sweet—he'd thought of everything. As he pulled out his tablet and an extra-long charging cord, she pulled out the chair next to the table.

"There's only one chair," Mike protested. "Let's use the bed. We can prop pillows behind our backs and put the tablet between us. More comfortable for both of us."

She had to admit that was the most practical thing to do. Since Lira was sacked out on the bed they'd shared last night, leaving it rather damp and smelling of wet dog, she grabbed all the pillows and crawled into Mike's bed, arranging the pillows comfortably.

Mike moved to stand by the bed, smiling down at her. "Move over, darling?"

Her heart leapt into her throat. "Wha-at?"

"How about some monkey business?"

She could only gape at him. Was he really suggesting—

"The movie," he said, toeing off his shoes to join her on the bed. "I know you like Rock Hudson and Cary Grant. Do you want to watch *Move Over, Darling* or *Monkey Business?*"

Oh! Her face flamed hot, but from his amused expression, he must have done it deliberately. "Seeing as how you're a Danny Kaye fan, how about *Court Jester?*"she shot back.

"*Some Like It Hot?*" he countered.

"*Dumb and Dumber.*"

He chuckled and brought up the Netflix app on his tablet. "What's the matter? A little *High Anxiety* giving you *Vertigo?*"

Hitchcock, huh? "*Psycho,*" she accused.

He laughed out loud. "What would you really like to see?"

"How about binge-watching *Friends?*"

He slid her a rueful glance. "Okay, I'll go along with that. For now."

For now? Her heart leapt into her throat. What did that mean? And, even more important, what did she want it to mean?

✿ ✿ ✿ ✿

HOURS LATER, after they had watched way too many movies, and binged on popcorn and hot chocolate, Mike gazed down at Kat affectionately. His flirtation had obviously flustered her, so he'd toned it down, and she'd relaxed into the Kat he remembered. She was lying on her side, facing him, while Lira stirred restlessly in the other bed.

He didn't know when he'd enjoyed a day as much as he'd enjoyed this one. Just being with Kat was a treat. He never knew what she was going to say or do next. And, despite her accusing him of being a stick-in-the-mud, he really enjoyed her spontaneity.

As the movie they were watching ended, he slid the tablet off the pillow they'd propped it on and moved to lie on his side, facing her. "I don't know about you, but I'm a bit movie'd out."

"I never thought I'd say this, but I am too."

He tucked a stray curl behind her ear. "This is nice—just like old times." Better, actually, since it was just the two of them, so close they were almost touching, and Kat finally seemed more aware of him as a man instead of just a friend.

She nodded and smiled happily, snuggling into the pillow.

"Except for your mom coming to check on us and Goldie trying to hog all the attention."

He chuckled. "I think Mom wanted to make sure we didn't do anything . . . intimate. She constantly gave me lectures about you."

"She did?" Kat raised up on an elbow in surprise. "Huh. Little did she know we didn't even think of doing anything . . . you know."

Well, maybe she hadn't, but he'd been a typical randy teenager and constantly thought about "you know." The only difference was, he hadn't let Kat know it—Mom's lectures kept him in line. He made a noncommittal noise.

She smiled and tapped his nose playfully. "If we were at your house, we could play Battleship, or—" She broke off suddenly with a strangled "Eek!" and thrust her pelvis toward him.

Mike gaped at her in astonishment. He didn't know how to play "Eek," but if it involved thrusting hips, he was certainly willing to try it.

She scrambled off the bed and pulled down her sweater which had ridden up in the back. Scrubbing Lira's ears, she said, "Your nose is very cold on bare skin, sweetie."

Mike laughed ruefully. "I wondered what that was all about."

Kat gave him an apologetic glance. "I think she's bored. She wants to go outside."

"We can't chance that."

"I know. She's been good about using the piddle pad, but she probably needs some exercise. I'd better play with her for a while."

Mike sighed. Moment ruined. Well, with any luck, there would be more chances to get past Kat's guard and show her how good they could be together.

CHAPTER ELEVEN

After Kat played with Lira, they watched more movies and turned in after shoving the damp bedspread to the floor. There was nothing else to do, really. Or, at least, nothing she was willing to do. She was a little wary of this new, playful, seductive Mike, but he was also courteous and helpful, just like always. She wasn't sure how to react to him, but resolved to treat him like she had when they were kids.

The only problem was, they were no longer kids. . . .

The next morning, they ditzed around until the sun came out enough to melt some of the snow and the snow plows had time to do their thing. Kat was beginning to feel cabin fever herself. They turned on the news to find out more about the weather.

After giving a list of school closings and business delays, they reported, "I-25 is clear, but icy. If you don't have to go out, stay home."

"We have to go out," Kat reminded Mike, afraid he would keep them in this room for another day.

He nodded. "We will. We'll take it slow and be careful."

"In other news," the reporter said, "famous movie canine

Lira is still missing. She was last seen in the company of this woman, who is suspected of stealing her." Kat and Lira's pictures flashed up on the screen. "Lira's owner is offering a reward for any information on finding the famous dog. If you have any knowledge of her whereabouts—"

Horrified, Kat scrambled for the television remote and clicked off the news. "They posted my picture." Panic rose within her. "Like I'm a criminal or something."

"It's okay," Mike said as he pulled her in for a hug. "Don't worry. Everything will be fine."

She shoved him away, unwilling to be comforted when she knew damn well she was right. "You don't know that. And you can't guarantee nothing will happen to me." She felt all the blood rush from her head and covered her cheeks with her hands. "I'm going to jail." And it was all her own fault. She glared at him, daring him to say her impulsiveness had brought her to this point.

"Let's just take one day at a time, shall we?" Mike said. "Tell you what—while you put your wig on and keep Lira hidden, I'll pack the car so we can head for Sanctuary."

"That's not going to keep me from going to jail," she protested.

"Maybe not," he said gently, "but it will get Lira to safety. Isn't that why you did this in the first place?"

Kat glanced down at the sweet dog, who was chewing on her rope again. "I suppose." But it was so unfair when she was in the right. Renewed determination to save the dog filled her. "You're right." Mike usually was, to her chagrin. "Let's get Lira to safety. We'll worry about the rest of it later." What would be, would be, and she'd face the consequences of her actions. After all, Lira was the important thing here.

Kat took Lira into the bathroom and made a silly-looking topknot with the blue ribbons on the dog, then put the wig on herself and slathered on enough make-up to totally change her appearance. She didn't wear much as a rule, so she applied the eye shadow, eye liner, and blush with a heavy hand. She looked at the result critically. Okay, she didn't look much like herself anymore, and though she felt like a clown, the make-up actually looked like it fit with this hairstyle. As with dying Lira's hair, the wig and make-up changed Kat's whole appearance. Who was this person? With the dark bob, heavy bangs, and exotic make-up, she looked more like a femme fatale than a dog trainer.

Just to complete the look, she put on one of those feminine blouses and clingy knit pants Aimee had brought, that accentuated her . . . assets.

Mike knocked on the door. "Ready to go?"

"Sure." Kat grabbed her things, shoved them in the bags, and opened the door.

Mike took a step back. "Wow. That's . . . quite a change."

Suddenly self-conscious, Kat asked, "It's not too much, is it?"

"No, I'd say it's just right. You look nothing like the picture on the news."

Relieved, Kat said, "Good. We're ready to go."

"I parked the car right in front of the door. Let me just check outside to make sure no one else is around, then we can go."

Kat nodded and cleaned up Lira's piddle pad and took it, along with all evidence of the dye job, out to a nearby dumpster, then Mike quickly took the dog out the door and into the waiting car. Kat stared in dismay at the bright red Jeep Cherokee. "I didn't realize Aimee's car was quite so . . . noticeable."

"It's kind of a common car, but . . . would you rather take the van?" he asked. "Or we could rent something nondescript, but it would be on file with my name on it."

The van was out—with the vet sign on the side, it would

be asking for trouble. And she didn't want anyone to be able to trace them through a car rental, either. "No, I guess not," she said reluctantly.

"Hey, you know what they say about hiding in plain sight," Mike said, obviously trying to buck her up.

"That you're more likely to get caught?" she countered.

"No, that it looks less suspicious," he said. "Come on, Kat. We don't have a choice. Let's get going."

Kat sighed. He was right, darn it—she didn't have a choice. Pulling her coat more snugly around her, she got in the car.

As they pulled away, Lira nosed Mike, trying to get him to open the window.

"No," Mike told the dog. "It's too cold, and hanging your head out the window is too risky."

Kat gave her the cue to lie down. Lira didn't like it, but she obeyed.

"It's for your own good," Kat told the disappointed dog.

Mike took it slow and easy, and eased onto the interstate. He drove well below the speed limit, and though it made her a bit impatient, Kat had to admit it was safer this way. The snow plows had done a good job, but there was still black ice in spots. It wouldn't do for them to get halfway to safety, only to wind up in a wreck on the highway.

When they got to South Academy Blvd, Mike said, "This is our exit. There's a Walmart here. Need anything?"

"No, let's just keep moving."

"Okay, but I need to stop for gas first. There aren't that many places along Highway 115 to fill up."

Kat nodded and glanced at Lira, who was getting restless. "Think I can risk taking her out to do her business?"

Mike frowned. "You should be okay, but make it quick."

When they stopped, Kat hustled Lira out of the car and over to a bare patch of snow nearby. With all the snow, there wasn't any grass showing. It was harder for Lira to find just the right spot, but she finally did, and Kat cleaned up the mess. As she headed back to the car, Mike glanced at them, looking worried.

"Sh—*he* had to find just the right spot," Kat explained when she got to the car, conscious of the other customers filling their tanks.

Mike nodded, and raised his hand toward his head.

No! Kat leapt forward and grabbed his arm before he could complete the motion. Noticing strange looks from another customer, she thought quickly. "You told me to stop you when you . . . start to bite your nails," she said with a mocking wag of her finger.

"Uh, yeah, right," Mike said with a grimace. "Thanks. Shall we get going?"

"I'm ready."

As they pulled away, Lira safely ensconced in the back seat, Mike said, "I'm sorry. I almost totally screwed up there."

"It's okay," Kat assured him, though the adrenaline surge left her heart racing like a greyhound. Truth be told, it was good to see Mike mess up every once in a while. Made her feel less like an idiot herself. "How long will it take to get to Dogwood?"

"Normally, about forty-five minutes from here, but in these conditions, it might take twice as long."

Of course it would. Everything else had taken much longer than she'd expected. Why couldn't she have kidnapped Lira in the summer? Everything would have been so much easier. She glanced at Mike. Then again, she might not have reconnected with her best friend, either. "At least we can relax a bit once we get her to Sanctuary."

Mike nodded. "So, tell me what you've been doing since you left college."

She grimaced. Why? So he could condescend about her weird, short-term jobs? "Just piddly stuff. Why?"

That came out more surly and suspicious than she expected, so she wasn't surprised when Mike shot her a questioning glance. "It's been a long time since I've seen you, and I haven't heard from you in all that time. I just wondered what's been going on in your life. You know, like *friends* do.'"

"Sorry—reflex action. My parents always give me hell about my strange jobs and 'settling down,' so it's kind of a sore point with me."

"I'm not judging you. I'm just curious. When you left college here, did you go back to California?"

"Yes, I had no choice." Nowhere else to go.

"Did you finish school somewhere else?"

"No. I realized I wasn't cut out to be a vet. I couldn't stand it when animals were in pain or suffering. Not even long enough to help them." When Mike didn't condemn her for her decision, she added, "I worked for the humane society for a while, but their policy of euthanizing unwanted pets if they didn't get adopted within a certain period of time . . . well, I just couldn't take it."

"I understand. It's a tough decision they have to make."

"Then I had a number of other jobs. I worked in a pet store for a while." Until the manager's gross incompetence and bullying made her leave. "I worked at a zoo, too." But the menial jobs they had her do didn't satisfy her need to help the animals in the cages. "I also did some stints as a groomer and dog walker, which led to some assistant jobs in animal wrangling."

"Wrangling?"

"In Hollywood. You know—bringing animals to sets, ensuring they perform, keeping them groomed, teaching them tricks. That's how I got the job with Edward. It was the best job I ever had and I learned a lot about training dogs. I was hoping to set up my own animal-wrangling business, but I guess that's not going to happen now."

"You never know," Mike said, obviously trying to cheer her up.

Yeah, right. Who'd hire her after this stunt?

But thinking about the future was depressing, so she changed the subject. "How about you? What have you been doing?"

"Finished school, joined a vet practice. That's pretty much it."

She shot him an annoyed glance. "You make it sound so boring."

"It's not, really. It's a great job."

When he didn't elaborate, she said, "Tell me about your work with Sanctuary. How are you involved with them, again?"

"They're pretty well-known in the animal community for their humanitarian efforts. They help sponsor trips to rescue puppy mill dogs, take in unwanted pets, and rehabilitate them to help them find good homes. They have some good sponsors, but I like to support them by providing veterinarian services a couple of times a month."

Interesting—he seemed a lot more passionate about his volunteer work than his paying job. "They need them that often?" Kat asked, surprised.

Mike grimaced. "You'd be surprised by the condition some of these mill dogs arrive in. The dogs they keep for breeding are kept in horrible conditions—wire cages under their feet, no protection from the weather, and the cages are hosed down to clean them with the dogs still inside. Most arrive at the shelter with matted fur, rotting teeth, and some with missing eyes due to the high-pressure hoses."

"How horrible. How could someone do that to a defense-less animal?"

He sighed. "Unfortunately, the puppy mill owners only care about money—selling the cute puppies of tortured parents to pet stores."

"So they don't get any love?" Every living thing deserved love, especially animals dependent on humans for their survival.

He shook his head sadly. "No. When they outlive their usefulness, they're auctioned off like so much excess trash."

"That's horrible. Why doesn't the government get involved and shut them down?"

"Because their conditions meet the minimum standard for a dog breeding operation. When Sanctuary learns of a puppy mill that doesn't, they shut them down, but the lowlifes just start up somewhere else."

"What's to keep someone else from doing the same thing with the dogs Sanctuary rescues?" she asked in dismay.

"Well, for one thing, Sanctuary has a group of volunteers who closely screen each new pet parent, to ensure they'll be able to provide a safe, loving home for a rescue dog—and they require that each dog be neutered or spayed first, so they can't be bred again. That's where I come in—the pro bono work I mentioned."

"Good for you," Kat exclaimed. "But those poor dogs— they must really be traumatized."

"They are," he said grimly. "Most of them have never felt a kind human touch until they reach Sanctuary, or had a soft bed, or toys. Which is why they also ensure the prospective pet parents know and understand their potential emotional problems."

Kat shook her head. "That's horrible. Makes me want to rush right in and hug all of them."

He smiled at her. "Luckily, most of the residents of Dogwood feel the same way you do. There's no shortage of volunteers to help out, but they always welcome more."

It sounded like her kind of place, but unfortunately, she had no idea what would happen to her after all this was over. "Tell me more about the rescued dogs."

For the next hour and a half, he regaled her with stories about terrified dogs who had learned to trust people again after being adopted into loving homes. But as they neared the turn-off to Dogwood on Highway 50, she saw flashing lights.

"Oh, no. There's a roadblock. Do you think it's because of Lira?"

Mike frowned. "I'm not sure, but if we turn around now, it would look suspicious. Don't worry—you and Lira both look totally different. I doubt they'll make the connection."

Kat fidgeted until they were signaled to stop. She grabbed Mike's phone and pretended to be absorbed in whatever was on the screen, leaning forward to let the wig obscure her face.

Mike rolled down the window. "What's going on, Officer?"

"Mornin', folks," the man in uniform said. "I'm afraid there's been a bad accident on Highway 50 and the road is closed. You'll have to turn around."

Turn around? Crap. So close, and yet so far.

"Do you know how long it will take to clear it?" Mike asked.

"No, sorry, sir. It's a bad one, and there's traffic backed up, so it may take hours. Plus it's treacherous on the road. I recommend you turn around and try again tomorrow."

"All right," Mike said. "We'll do that. Thanks."

He rolled the window back up and turned around at the officer's direction.

Kat slugged him in the arm. "Why'd you do that?"

He gave her an annoyed look. "You heard him. We have no choice. And there really isn't a back way into Dogwood."

"What are we going to do now?" she asked, her voice rising. "We can't go back to the Springs."

"Don't panic," he reassured her. "We passed a campground a couple of miles back."

"Like that'll help," she scoffed. "Unless you have a tent and sleeping bags packed in back." Though she wouldn't put it past him—Mike had been a Boy Scout. But it was too cold for camping.

"They advertised cabins for rent as well," he soothed her. "We'll be fine."

Fifteen minutes later, they pulled into the campground. The office was in what looked like a log cabin, and there were even some hardy folks outside under a pavilion roasting marshmallows and drinking hot mugs of something and laughing and having a good old time. She shivered at the thought. No way would she join them.

Mike got out and went into the office as she rolled down the window a bit for Lira and stewed. Each delay made her even more nervous and afraid they'd never get the dog to safety. "Don't panic," he'd said. Well, that was all well and good for mellow Mike, but she was more realistic.

Finally, Mike emerged from the office and got back in the car.

"So, do we have a cabin?"

"Afraid not. They're all full up because of the road closure and the snow." And, being Mike, he did what he always did when he was nervous or frustrated—he shoved his hand through his hair.

"A-roo-roooo," Lira caroled out the open window, looking very pleased with herself.

As the people in the pavilion turned to stare, Kat snapped, "Now can I panic?"

CHAPTER TWELVE

MIKE QUICKLY PUT the car in reverse and got out of there, but he wasn't moving fast enough for Kat. "Hurry," she said, cuing Lira to lie down as Kat hid her own face.

"You *want* to look guilty?" he asked in exasperation.

"No, I just don't want to lose Lira." The more time went on, the more certain she was that if anyone stopped them, Lira wouldn't survive being returned to her owner.

"Well, they may not know it was Lira, and I don't want to arouse their suspicions." He turned right out of the campground, still going too darned slow.

"Where are you going? The highway is in the other direction."

"And that's where they'll expect us to go."

"But you don't even know what's out this way," she protested.

"Actually, I do. Don't worry—I have a plan."

"You do?" She was glad one of them did.

"Yes. I have a friend who lives out this way."

"Out in the middle of nowhere?"

He cast her an amused glance. "It's not nowhere to him.

He boards and trains horses, and I help him out now and again with vet care."

"Why didn't you think of this place before?"

"Because I didn't want to get him involved in something that might make him an accessory to a crime."

"Oh." She winced inwardly. She didn't really want to involve anyone else, but what choice did they have?

Mike pulled his phone from his pocket. "Here—go to my contacts and call Clint Hardison, then put the call on speaker so I can talk to him."

Now that she had something concrete to do, she calmed down a little. She did as he asked and soon heard a man's voice on the line. "Hello."

"Hi, Clint. This is Mike Duffy."

"Hey, Mike. What's going on?"

"Well, I'm in a spot and I hope you can help."

Mike wasn't going to tell Clint about Lira, was he? Kat's eyes widened and she held her hand up, waving frantically for him to stop.

He grimaced at her and shook his head impatiently.

Clint seemed to hesitate. "Well, I've got a problem myself at the moment, but if I can help, I will. What's up?"

"I was on my way to Dogwood with one of my assistants, Ka—Katie," Mike said, and Kat relaxed at this indication Mike wasn't going to reveal anything that might jeopardize Lira. "But the road's closed due to an accident. The cabins at the campground near you are all full up, so I was hoping we could stay in your guest house until the road opens again."

"You're near here now?" Clint asked, his voice sharpening.

"Yes—very close."

"Good. I'm in need of some help right now myself."

"What's the problem?"

"I think Cinnamon has colic. Can you check her out for me?"

"Of course. We'll be there in five."

"Good. I'm in the barn."

Mike nodded at Kat to hang up and she did so, asking, "What's colic?" She'd heard of babies having it, but didn't think Clint would ask for a vet's help with an infant in a barn.

"It's basically gastrointestinal pain. In this case, in a horse."

Relieved, she said, "So it's not serious, then?"

He shrugged as he turned off the road at a sign saying HARDISON HORSE BOARDING AND TRAINING. "Sometimes it's just like gas or constipation in a human. Other times, it can be an intestinal blockage or twisting of the intestines and requires immediate surgery."

"Can you do that here?"

"No—we'd have to take the horse somewhere that has the facilities for equine surgery. There are some in the area."

"I see." Kat didn't want the poor horse to suffer, but she didn't want Mike to have to make the choice between helping her and getting the horse to surgery either.

Mike found the turn-off to Clint's place and drove carefully up the snow-packed drive to the barn where a man stood in the doorway, waving at them. Tall, lean, and rangy, wearing a heavy coat and hat, the cowboy stood awkwardly on a pair of crutches, his right leg in a cast.

Mike got out of the car, and Kat followed as he got his medical bag out of the back, letting Lira out to sniff excitedly at all the new smells. "Remember," Mike said softly. "Your name is Katie."

She resisted the urge to roll her eyes, knowing he was just being thorough.

"Good to see you, Clint," Mike said with a handshake. "This is my assistant, Katie, and her dog . . ."

"Bruiser," Kat supplied quickly with the first masculine-sounding name she could think of. "But he's a sweetheart and very well-trained. Come here, *boy*," she said to Lira, "and shake hands."

She gave Lira a cue, and she obediently lifted her paw toward Clint.

He chuckled and solemnly shook her paw. "Nice to meet you, Bruiser. And you, too, ma'am." Now that she was closer, she could see the man had a devastating smile and a pair of twinkling blue eyes that probably caused a lot of female hearts to go pitty-pat. He was polite, too. Nice.

Mike must have felt the need to explain Lira, because he added, "Ka—Katie thought Bruiser needed an outing, so we brought . . . him with us."

"How is he with horses?" Clint asked Kat doubtfully.

"He's very well-behaved," she assured him.

He nodded. "I just don't want him to get hurt. Come on in. Don't stand out there in the cold."

They followed him into the warm barn, and, as Clint swung out on his crutches, Mike asked, "What happened to you?"

Clint shook his head. "Sheer stupidity. I slipped on the ice yesterday morning and broke my leg."

Ouch. Kat winced in sympathy.

Mike glanced around. "And you're alone?"

Clint came to a stop in front of a stall, looking as though the effort had caused him pain. "Yes. The trainer and groom are at a horse show, and I gave the stablehands the weekend off, figuring I could manage for a couple of days on my own." He grimaced. "I didn't count on breaking my leg, or Cinnamon coming down with colic. They're snowbound right now at a ski resort and the pass is closed, so they probably won't be able to come back until tomorrow. I was getting ready to beg for a neighbor's help when you called." He nodded toward the stall. "Can you check her out? She hasn't been eating and hasn't . . ." He slanted a glance at Kat and apparently changed his mind about what he was going to say. "Hasn't had a bowel movement in a while."

"Of course."

Mike moved into the stall with his bag, and Kat gave Lira the cue to sit and stay out of the way. Kat peered over the edge of the stall and saw a reddish-brown mare shifting restlessly, pawing at the floor as if she were in pain.

"I tried walking her," Clint added, "but it didn't seem to relieve her distress. I didn't know how I was going to get her in the trailer and to the local vet by myself."

Kat glanced at him in surprise. He'd walked the horse? That couldn't have been easy on crutches. No wonder Clint looked exhausted and in pain.

"It's okay, old girl," Mike soothed her with a caress of her neck. "We're going to find out what's wrong with you."

Kat watched as Mike moved efficiently around Cinnamon, checking her vitals, feeling her sides, listening to her belly with a stethoscope, and taking her temperature rectally.

Ewww. That didn't look like fun for either Mike *or* the horse.

But she had to admit she was impressed. Mike really knew what he was doing.

Clint frowned in concern. "Is it serious?"

"Doesn't look like it will require surgery," Mike said, smiling. "More like gas or impaction. You have mineral oil on hand, don't you? And a nasogastric tube?"

"I do," Clint said with relief. "I thought I might need some, so I have a bucket of oil warmed up, along with some warm water. They're in the tack room." He turned as if to head there, but Kat stopped him.

"Just tell me where they are, and I'll get them."

"We both will," Mike said. Then, to Clint, he said, "Just stay here with Cinnamon, keep her calm."

Clint nodded, and Mike led her to the tack room where he rummaged around until he found some tubing and a pump. "Have you really been around horses before?" he asked quietly.

"A few times, on sets, and I took horseback riding lessons in California."

He paused for a moment, then seemed to come to a decision. "I'll need your help to take care of Cinnamon."

"My help? What can *I* do?"

"Normally, I'd have Clint help me hold the horse's head still, but I'm not sure he's steady enough on those crutches to do it by himself."

Yeah, but she had no doubt the man would try—he was obviously concerned for his horse. "I can do that," she said with more confidence than she felt. She owed Mike that much.

Mike carried the buckets back to the stall while she brought the tubing and pump. After Mike hooked the thing up, he told Clint, "Katie's in training and hasn't worked with horses much yet, but she'll do fine."

Kat nodded. "Just tell me what to do."

"Here, ma'am, I'll show you."

Clint showed her where to stand and how to hold the halter with a light, relaxed grip. "Don't let her toss her head." He grabbed the water bucket as well as an empty one and passed them to Mike. He stroked Cinnamon's neck. "It's all right, girl. You've done this before. You'll feel better soon."

Kat watched curiously as Mike expertly placed the tube in the horse's nose. "I'm going to feed the tube into her stomach," he explained. "Then we'll pump some water into it." He did that with a metal hand pump.

Cinnamon didn't seem to care for the procedure, but she held relatively still for it as Kat held her halter in a death grip, keeping her head still.

"Not much reflux," Mike said as some liquid came back up out of the stomach and he directed it into an empty bucket. "That's a good sign."

"What do we do now?" Kat asked.

As Clint poured a gallon jug of oil into another bucket, Mike said, "We give her some mineral oil—it acts like a laxative."

He did the pumping action again until the bucket was empty. "Now we wait for the laxative to work."

Oh, lovely.

Mike pulled the tube from the horse's nose and gave her a pat. The whole procedure hadn't taken more than ten minutes. "And I'll give her a shot of Banamine to reduce the inflammation."

Well, at least the poor horse hadn't required surgery. And Cinnamon looked like she was feeling better already—she wasn't nearly as restless.

"Watch her for us," Mike said, "while I help Clint clean up here."

Kat nodded as Mike grabbed the buckets and headed off with Clint. She watched the horse, not sure what she should be looking for, but figured if Cinnamon did anything different, she could call Mike.

From the sounds of things, he was helping with more than just the buckets. No doubt the poor cowboy had had problems doing normal chores around the stable with his broken leg.

Helping Clint just proved once more how nice Mike was. Not to mention incredibly competent. He'd been so sure, calm, and confident in everything he'd done, keeping not only the horse calm, but her owner and his "assistant" as well. Mike was a really good vet, she realized. And a really good man.

When she'd first seen the sexy cowboy standing in the

doorway, she'd been impressed by his lean physique, broad shoulders, and good looks. But now that Clint and Mike were standing side by side, she noticed Mike had the same body type. And, if she was honest, he was even better-looking than Clint. Holy cow. That was a stunner.

She knew he'd grown up to realize potential she never knew he had, but she hadn't really noticed until now that he was a real hottie. She stared for a moment, open-mouthed, then quickly admonished herself to forget it—Mike was a friend, nothing more.

Instead, she turned her mind to something else, like her future . . . if she even had one. She bit her lip, trying to figure out how to come out of this relatively unscathed, and realized she hadn't a clue. She'd just have to play it by ear and hope everything worked out.

After about half an hour of fruitless worrying, the horse lifted her tail. Kat craned her neck to see what was going on, then realized what she was doing.

"Hey, Mike," she called out in excitement, "Cinnamon's taking a dump."

Mike looked up and grinned at her, and she couldn't help but laugh at herself. Who knew she'd be so excited about horse dung?

CHAPTER THIRTEEN

MIKE HAD to grin at Kat's enthusiasm. She'd seemed energized by helping with the simple procedure, but Clint looked exhausted and as if his leg was paining him. Time for Clint to get some rest, Mike decided. "Cinnamon should be okay for now, but I'll continue to check on her. You need to rest your leg."

Clint nodded. "Thanks, Mike. I owe you one."

Mike shook his head. "Naw, letting us stay in the guest house will more than repay us."

They helped him back to the house and into the living room where his two Labrador retrievers gave Lira the traditional butt-sniffing greeting, but were polite enough to welcome her as a guest by the fireplace. Kat slid off her coat and glanced around at the homey, rustic place. "Very nice. Did your wife decorate it herself?"

Mike gave her a sharp glance. Why the blatant attempt at finding out if Clint was married?

Clint glanced appreciatively at the curves Kat had revealed. "No, ma'am. I'm not married. The decorating would be my sister's doing. But I'll tell her you liked it."

Mike had had enough of their little flirtation. "Can we wash our hands somewhere?"

Clint nodded. "There's a sink there," he told Kat, pointing to the guest bathroom with a crutch. "And Mike can use the one in the kitchen."

Kat headed toward the bathroom, and Clint hobbled after Mike as he walked toward the kitchen. Feeling guilty, Mike said, "Sit, man, sit. You've been standing too long, and that's gotta be uncomfortable."

"I will in a moment," Clint said as Mike soaped his hands. "But I'm a mite hungry and I figure you two are as well. My sister left a tray of lasagna for me, and I want to put it in the oven." He rummaged around in the refrigerator while Mike finished washing his hands. He wiped his hands on the nearby towel then went to help Clint. Dealing with crutches and a pan of lasagna wouldn't be easy.

"Thanks," Clint said as Mike took it from him. "She left instructions for heating it on top."

Mike nodded and put the pan in the oven.

Kat came in. "Is that lunch?" she asked.

"Yes, ma'am. I hope you like lasagna."

"Who doesn't?" Kat said with a grin.

As Clint continued to limp around the kitchen, Mike said, "You need to take some weight off that injury. Sit, put your leg up, and let us do that for you."

"Mike's right," Kat said. "Hold on, let me get you something to cushion your leg."

She rushed back into the living room and came back with a throw pillow, which she placed on one of the kitchen chairs. "Here, use this."

Clint nodded and eased down into another chair then rested his calf on the pillow. "Thank you. That helps."

Kat beamed at him. "Just tell us where everything is, and we'll get it out for you."

How very helpful of her, Mike thought with a snarky edge. She hadn't ever been that solicitous with *him*. Was she interested in his friend? And why did that make Mike so grumpy? He'd have to warn her off. Clint wasn't the love-'em-and-leave-'em type she usually dated.

Clint gave them directions on where to find the dishes and silverware, then explained where the bread and salad fixings were.

"I'll make the salad if you'll take care of the bread," Mike told Kat. Cooking was one of those things he really enjoyed doing and, judging from what Kat had admitted about the state of her refrigerator a few days ago, it wasn't really her thing.

Some of the strain on Clint's face eased as he rested his leg. When the oven timer dinged, Mike took the pan out and Clint told Kat, "There's a pitcher of iced tea in the fridge."

She nodded and they put it all on the table. Soon, they were chowing down, and Mike was glad to have something to eat besides sandwiches.

"So," Clint said to Kat, "what do you think about your first time working with a horse?"

Kat grinned. "I liked it. I love working with animals, and haven't worked with horses before. Do you need an extra hand around here?" she asked impulsively.

Clint glanced at Mike with a question in his eyes.

Mike forced a chuckle. "You already have a job," he reminded her. Even if it was imaginary, Clint didn't know that. "And, no worries, we'll work with horses often enough, as well as household pets."

Kat gave him an apologetic glance. Evidently, she'd forgotten about their deception in her enthusiasm for helping with Cinnamon.

Changing the subject, Mike asked Clint, "How's business with horse boarding and training these days?"

As Clint talked about his business, Kat kept quiet, looking chastened. Once they finished eating, Kat and Mike cleaned up, not allowing Clint to help. The man was stubborn, though, and would continue to try to play host unless Mike gave him a reason not to.

He put the last dish in the dishwasher and turned to Clint. "I take it the guest house is free?"

Clint nodded. "It's yours for as long as you want it."

Kat gave Mike an odd look. "The road might be cleared by now."

"It might, but I'd like to keep an eye on Cinnamon until the morning, and give Clint a hand with the horses." He turned to his friend. "You said your help would be back sometime tomorrow?"

"They should be."

"Then if it's all right, we'll stay the night in the guest house and leave tomorrow morning." At Clint's nod, Mike added, "And don't worry—I know where it is, and we can find our way around the guest house without your help. You stay here and rest that leg."

Clint seemed relieved, but still insisted on getting up and showing them to the door. Kat cued Lira to come, remembering to not use her name, and the dog came bounding over. "I'll check on Cinnamon first," Mike told Clint. "And if you let me know when the horses need to be fed next, I'll do that too."

When Clint started to protest, Mike said, "Give yourself time to heal, man. The sooner you do that, the sooner you'll be able to get back to full function."

Clint nodded. "Thank you. The guest house isn't locked."

Mike checked on Cinnamon first. The mare seemed to be feeling better, and he could hear the sounds of her gut moving, so he was confident the colic episode was over.

Walking back to their borrowed SUV, he said, "I'll just pull the car closer so we can bring a few things in."

Once they were settled in the small cabin, Kat said, "Well, if we're not going anywhere else today, I can get out of this disguise. This wig itches."

She disappeared into the bathroom and, noticing the fireplace had already been thoughtfully set up, he lit a fire and set up his tablet on a small table in front of the couch.

When she emerged, her face had been scrubbed clean of all make-up and she was scratching her mop of blond curls. He smiled. Now that was the Kat he knew and remembered.

"Oh, that's nice," she said when she spotted the fire. Lira, naturally, had claimed a spot in front of the fireplace and lay down with a sigh of contentment.

As Kat settled in next to him on the couch, she said, "I'm sorry about my slip back there. I wasn't thinking."

Mike bit back a sigh. Her mantra. "What *were* you thinking?"

She shrugged. "Just that I'll probably need a job once this is all over—if I'm not in jail—and I kind of liked working with the horse."

"Liked working with Clint, you mean," Mike said.

"He's okay," she said off-handedly.

"Okay?" he repeated. "Then what was all that flirting and 'Do you have a wife?' stuff about?"

She raised her eyebrows. "He said his crew was gone, but I was just trying to figure out if anyone else was around the house."

Yeah, right. "Why?"

"Because the fewer people who see Lira and me, the better."

Hmph. She had a point. "Well, it seemed like more than that to me."

"It wasn't," she reassured him. Then, giving him a ques-

117

tioning look, she asked, "So what if it was? Are you saying you wouldn't want your friend dating me?"

No, he didn't, but he wasn't prepared to admit that to her. "I just don't want to have to pick up the pieces when you realize you're all wrong for each other."

"Who are you to judge?" Her eyes flashed annoyance. "What, you think you're Cupid now, with special knowledge on who should be together? Or that matchmaking dog?"

"No," Mike said softly. "It's just that I've picked up the pieces too many times after yet another man has broken your heart. I don't want to have to do it again."

She threw her hands up in the air. "So, what? I'm never allowed to date again, in case Mike Duffy might have to pretend to be my friend, let me cry on his shoulder?"

He didn't even know how to respond to that. "That's not what I meant, and you know it. I don't want to see you hurt again."

She seemed mollified and her anger dissipated as fast as it had arisen. She sighed. "I wasn't really, you know, all those times. It wasn't my heart that was hurting—it was my pride."

"Oh, Kat." Mike's heart hurt at her admission, and he unthinkingly pulled her in for a one-armed hug.

Big mistake. She curled into his chest as if she belonged there—all trusting, warm, and soft. He resisted the urge to squeeze her tight.

Sighing against his chest, she said, "I missed you, you know."

Hope flooded through him, but he beat it back down. "I missed you, too."

"Let's not lose touch again, okay?"

What? And have her continue to treat him like the boy next door? A handy, genderless confidante? He didn't know if he could continue to play that role forever.

"Mike?" Kat asked when he remained silent.

He sighed. When could he ever refuse Kat? "Okay, sure." If this was the only way he could have her in his life, it would have to do. "Can you get up for a minute?"

She moved, looking questioningly at him, and he handed her the tablet. "Here—find something to watch while I check the news. Let's see how bad the situation is now." And what Clint would see if he watched a broadcast.

Mike watched the news as Kat scrolled through the movies available on Netflix. Thankfully, they didn't have any more information on Lira than had already been reported, and, judging from the reduced airtime the station gave the story, maybe the interest was dying down as well. He said as much to Kat.

She nodded. "You were right. It looks like the campers didn't recognize Lira or me. The disguises worked."

"At least the weather looks like it will be much better tomorrow, and the road is open."

"Yeah." She rolled her eyes. "Gee, it's only taking, what? Four days to go sixty miles?"

He laughed. "We should be there tomorrow, no problem."

They settled in to watch a couple of the romantic comedies Kat loved. Mike had to admit he enjoyed them as well, though life didn't always seem to work out as well or as neatly as they did in the movies.

When the movies ended, they ate some of the sandwiches Aimee had brought them, and he glanced outside to see night had fallen. "I need to check on Cinnamon, and feed the horses. I'll take *Bruiser* with me."

Kat grinned. "Don't you need help? I'm supposed to be your assistant, remember?"

"Do you really want to put your disguise back on?"

"Do I need to?"

"Hold on, I'll check." He texted quickly back and forth with Clint, to get instructions on what he was feeding the horses. It took some doing, but he finally convinced Clint that he and Kat could handle it on their own, and that the horses would be better served if Clint stayed in the house and healed.

"He's going to stay in the house and let us do this," Mike told her as he shrugged on his coat, "but you might want to put the wig on anyway, or a hat, just in case he looks out the window."

"Okay. This thing is as warm as a hat anyway."

She pulled the wig on, along with her coat, and called Lira. The dog bounded over enthusiastically and they headed out toward the barn.

All he heard was the crunch of their footsteps in the snow as they headed for the barn. Lira stuck close to Kat, her night vision impaired because of the disease.

Halfway there, Kat stopped.

"What's wrong?"

"Nothing," she said and threw her arms wide, her face to the sky. "Shh, just listen."

He halted, and a hush fell in the crisp, cold night air. The scent of wood smoke wafted on a light breeze, and out here, far from the city, there were few lights except for the moon and stars, and no signs of traffic.

"It's so quiet," she whispered. "So beautiful."

He stared at her in bemusement. He'd always thought of Kat as a city girl, but right now, she looked like some sort of pagan goddess petitioning the moon. "Beautiful," he agreed softly.

She stood that way for perhaps a minute longer, then released a sigh and lowered her arms. "Nature is good for the soul."

"It is."

She glanced mischievously up at him. "Well, come on. Those horses are probably hungry."

They headed into the warm barn and he checked Cinnamon first.

"How is she?" Kat asked in concern.

"Much better. We can feed her now."

"How do we do that?"

As Mike explained the dietary needs of the horses, Kat followed him enthusiastically, bubbling with questions and helping out where he needed it while Lira stayed out of the way. When he was almost done, Kat said, "While you finish up, I'm going to take Lira out. We've kept her cooped up a lot lately and she could use the exercise."

Mike nodded. "Good idea, but stay close."

She waved in acknowledgement and headed out the door. Once he finished up, she was waiting for them outside the door and walked with him back to the guest house.

Inside, they pulled off their coats and Kat jerked off the wig, then scrubbed her head vigorously. "I think I'll turn in. I'm a bit tired."

Mike nodded. "Me, too." It had been an exhausting day—mentally, if not physically. "I'll just build up the fire first."

She headed toward the bedroom, then stopped short. "There's only one bedroom," she said in confusion.

Yeah, he'd noticed that earlier. Without turning around, he said, "That's okay. I'll take the couch."

"Don't be silly. It's too short for you, and it's a bit lumpy. You wouldn't get much sleep. I'll take it."

He finished with the fire and rose to his feet to face her. "You want to sleep on a lumpy couch? Don't be ridiculous. You take the bed."

She shook her head, her lips pressed together in thought. "You know what? This is dumb. It's not like you're going to jump me or anything, right?"

The images that conjured up made Mike grit his teeth again and he managed to shake his head no.

"Then let's share the bed. It's king-sized and, knowing Lira, she'll want to be in between us anyway. That way we can both be comfortable and get a decent night's sleep."

"That sounds sensible." Mike grinned. "In Colonial days, unmarried couples often used bundling boards, sacks, or pillows laid down the center of a mattress so they could share a bed without coming into contact."

"So Lira's our bundling sack?" She seemed amused, which was what he'd hoped.

"Hey, whatever works." He moved to the side of the bed and pulled down the covers. "But I, uh, don't think it'll be very comfortable sleeping in jeans."

"Oh, yeah," Kat said, blushing. "What do you sleep in?"

"Just my boxers normally." And he certainly hadn't thought to bring pajama bottoms—not that he owned any.

"Uh, okay. Why don't I . . . turn off the light, and you can take off— I mean, you can get ready for bed while I change into my nightgown."

Aaaand the awkwardness was back.

"Okay," Mike said doubtfully, not sure this was a good idea. She was right about one thing, though—Lira jumped on the bed, turned around three times, and settled in the center. And that couch did look uncomfortable. Hell, why not torture himself?

"Okay," Kat said nervously. "Go ahead. I'll be right back." She flipped the light off and left the room.

Mike stripped off his clothes, all but his boxers, and laid them neatly on a nearby chair then climbed into bed next to Lira. "Hey, girl," he said softly as he rubbed her ears. "No offense, but I'd really rather share the bed with your trainer. Alone."

She licked his hand as if in apology and Mike sighed. The door opened and Kat was silhouetted briefly through her gown, backlit by the firelight, her womanly curves revealed to his avid gaze.

He groaned to himself as she settled herself on the bed. How the heck was he supposed to sleep with that image in his head, Kat's warm body lying a couple of feet away, and his own body begging him to play "Eek" with her?

CHAPTER FOURTEEN

KAT WOKE SLOWLY the next morning, feeling warm and comfy. Lira must have gotten cold in the middle of the night because she was spooned—

Wait. That wasn't Lira. Somehow, even in this big bed, she and Mike had gravitated toward each other like two magnets. Mike lay spooned against her backside, with his arm around her waist and their legs tangled together.

Kat knew she should get up, pretend this hadn't happened, but it was so nice lying here in the circle of his arms, even if it was a total accident. She felt warm, safe, loved. . . . When was the last time she'd felt this way?

Never. She'd never let herself get close enough to anyone, never trusted anyone not to abandon her, never trusted a relationship enough to let it run its course to the inevitable nasty conclusion. As she admitted to Mike yesterday, she'd never let anyone get close enough to really hurt her.

There was definitely some kind of chemistry between her and Mike. Should she act on it or not? On one hand, the chemistry was causing some tingling in places that hadn't tingled in way too long. On the other hand, she'd never find a friend as good as Mike. Was it better to give in to her hormones . . . or ignore this magnetization that was happening and remain friends?

Friends, definitely. Safer that way.

Sighing to herself, she started to pull away from him, but his arm tightened around her, holding her to him. The tingling spread, and she firmly told her traitorous body to behave. Yes, it was obvious Mike had become aware of her as a woman, but he was such a gentleman, she doubted he was doing this consciously.

Another pressure made itself known—this one in her bladder. Reluctantly, firmly, she peeled herself away from him and headed for the bathroom. But once again, that super-strong magnet drew her gaze back to the bed.

Mike was one good-looking man. Though the sheets obscured his lower half, his upper half was . . . quite nice. His chest was broad and lightly furred, with taut, firm skin, making him primo beefcake calendar fodder. His hair was mussed and all sexy-looking, and his eyes gleamed knowingly at her as his mouth curved in a slow, wicked smile.

Caught! Quickly, she looked away and headed for the bathroom. She stayed in there longer than she really needed to, trying to force her body into some semblance of propriety. A shower helped, and so did getting dressed and putting on her disguise. Donning the wig and the Katie persona made it easier to deal with Mike—like virtual armor.

When she emerged, she glanced warily in Mike's direction, then relaxed when she realized he'd pulled on jeans and a T-shirt and was staring at his phone.

He glanced up. "Clint is going to make us breakfast. I'll take a quick shower and we can join him."

Still embarrassed he'd caught her admiring him, Kat nodded. "Okay. I'll just, uh, take Lira out."

She shoved her coat on and rushed the dog out the door

before Mike could say anything more. The cold snap of the morning air slapped her fully awake, effectively dispelling any lingering warm tingles. She didn't know whether to be glad or sad.

Clint's two labs were outside and bounded over to greet Lira. Kat smiled as the three of them romped in the snow like puppies. Well, slush was more like it. The snow had partially melted, and it was supposed to be warmer today, so it looked like there would be no impediment to finally getting to Sanctuary.

Nothing, that was, but Mike's insistence they stay and help Clint out until he was sure his staff would arrive that evening.

When they finally got on the road after lunch, Kat sat quietly, lost in her thoughts.

Mike glanced at her. "Are you mad at me for staying so long?"

Kat waved his concern away. "Of course not. Clint obviously needed the help." And Mike was such a nice guy, he couldn't let his friend flounder.

"Then what's wrong?"

"Just thinking about . . . everything."

"Worried?" he asked softly.

"Yeah." The constant tension and worry about Lira was beginning to wear on her. Not to mention a niggling concern about her own future. "What's going to happen to me?" Even if she avoided going to jail, the chances of finding a job in the animal training industry were likely to be slim after this. And where would she live? What about her things?

She still had a lot of clothing and essentials in Lira's trailer and doubted Edward and Joey would hand them over easily. Thank goodness she'd left the bulk of her household goods in storage in California.

Mike covered her hand with his. "Everything will be all right, Kat. I promise."

How could he possibly promise that? He didn't have any control over the future. But, for some reason, his reassurance made her feel better. "I hope so."

They rode in silence on the freshly plowed road. Kat halfway expected a road block, but chided herself for being silly. Lira wasn't *that* important. All their roadblocks had been figurative so far—no reason to expect a literal one.

"This is it," Mike finally said, gesturing at the city-limit sign: WELCOME TO DOGWOOD—WHERE THE BEST THINGS IN LIFE ARE RESCUED.

Kat grinned as she relaxed even more. "I love that. I hope it's a sign."

Mike slanted a puzzled look at her. "What else would it be?"

"I mean I hope the sign is a sign." Realizing that didn't clarify anything, she added, "You know, a sign that Lira will be rescued for good."

"Ah. Well, we'll find out when we get to Sanctuary."

"Is it far?" Now that they were so close, she was getting excited.

"It's just north of town, so not too long."

Kat turned to pat Lira on the head. "We're almost there, sweetie."

He had to slow down as they drove through the town, since the roads here hadn't been cleared as well as the highway.

"What a quaint town," she exclaimed. The old brick buildings, Victorian architecture, and the charming town square made it look like something from a movie set. As they drove past the park in the center of the town square, she said, "Wait. That bronze statue. Is that what I think it is?"

Mike laughed. "I don't know. Do you think it looks like a dog peeing into a fountain?"

"Well, yeah." A Labrador retriever, to be specific.

"It is. Actually, the dog *is* the fountain. It was a gift to the town from Paul and Sandy McPherson, the founders of Sanctuary. The dog is a replica of Match, the first matchmaking dog in the town. They wanted to make sure that dogs have water on a hot summer's day—the dog statue, er, fills up the bowl beneath it. See that heart-shaped crystal on his chest?" When Kat nodded, he added, "That's where the heart-shaped blaze was on the first Match."

Oh, yeah, the matchmaking dog. Kat laughed. "I'm not sure I believe in the legend, but I like this town already."

"I knew you would."

They wound their way through the town, and, before long, came to a large wooden sign that read SADIE'S SANCTUARY.

Finally. "Who's Sadie?"

"Paul's former dog partner. Paul was a K-9 handler in Vietnam and wasn't allowed to bring her back with him, so he dedicated this place to her. But people here just call it Sanctuary now."

How sweet. But the weathered wooden sign was badly in need of a fresh paint job. She glanced at it doubtfully. "Looks kind of old."

"The sign may look neglected, but it doesn't reflect the rest of Sanctuary. They spend the money where it matters—on the animals."

Kat nodded, but reserved judgment.

Mike parked in the unpaved parking lot next to a number of large buildings. And, she noted approvingly, a number of fenced areas. Some dogs were in the nearest one and came running to bark at them.

Mike unbuckled his seat belt. "Probably best to leave Lira here for now."

She nodded. The day was sunny, and it was warm enough in the car. Typical of Colorado—a blizzard one day, and bright sunshine the next. Kat cracked her window to let some fresh air in, and exited the car.

She walked up to the chain-link fence to pet the dogs. Some happily licked her fingers, but others backed away, obviously fearful. "Those poor dogs."

"That's due to the puppy mills. They have no reason to trust people."

"That's so sad." Her heart broke for them.

"It is, but Sanctuary ensures they have a soft, warm bed, good food, toys, and people to love them. They have the best adoption rate in the state."

"What are all these buildings for?"

"This biggest one here is the main housing area for dogs. Others have cats, rabbits, goats, horses, and other animals. That one there," he said, pointing to the one behind the main area, "is a clinic where they care for the animals who have medical issues, and where I do the neutering once a month." When she nodded, he added, "And they have special areas where they keep dogs who need additional socialization before being adopted, another one for grooming, plus storage areas for donated food, etc."

"Quite an operation," Kat said admiringly. Apparently, these people really did care about animals. She'd brought Lira to the right place.

The door between the building and the fenced-in area opened and a woman stuck her head out. "Potty break is over. Time to come inside," she yelled.

Oh, good. The dogs didn't have to spend a lot of time out in the cold. Quickly, Kat checked to make sure her wig was in place.

The woman glanced over at them, then smiled widely. "Mike! So you're the reason why they're so boisterous. Let us get these guys settled, then I'll meet you in the greeting room."

Mike nodded and gestured for Kat to precede him into the building.

"Is that Sandy?" Kat asked once they were inside.

"No, it's her daughter, Amber. I won't introduce you until it's necessary."

Understanding he didn't want to lie to his friends, Kat nodded.

They entered the building and a wire-haired terrier came running up to them, obviously friendly and looking to be loved on.

"Well, this one doesn't need socialization," Kat said with a laugh as she leaned down to lavish attention on the dog.

"No, Scooter has designated himself as the official greeter," Mike said with a smile. "He's come a long way. You should have seen him when he first arrived."

After a few minutes, Amber yelled instructions to someone, then came back inside. She beamed at Mike, then gave him a big hug.

Now, seeing her up close, Kat realized the woman couldn't be old enough to have a husband who served in Vietnam. With thick golden hair and a beautiful smile, Amber looked to be about Kat's age and was very attractive. And she obviously thought Mike was, too. In fact, even after she stopped hugging him, she held onto his arm, as if afraid he'd take off without her. Or was she staking a claim?

Now that was a disturbing thought. Mike wasn't married, but he'd never said if he was seeing someone. Like Amber, maybe?

"We weren't expecting you, were we, Mike?" Amber gave Kat a curious glance. "Is your . . . friend looking to adopt?"

Mike hurried to answer. "No, I wasn't expected, but I am here to see Paul and Sandy. Are they here?"

"No, I'm sorry. They picked up some dogs in Kansas to take to another shelter, and haven't been able to make it back yet, due to the snow. Is it something I can help you with?" Once again, she turned her curious gaze on Kat.

Disappointment filled Kat. Another roadblock. Mike glanced at her with a questioning look. She assumed Mike was asking her if she wanted to trust Amber, but since the woman hadn't released her grip on Mike, Kat was feeling contrary. She shook her head slightly.

"Do you know when they'll be back?" he asked.

"Tomorrow sometime."

"Okay, we'll just wait until tomorrow."

"We?" Amber asked pointedly.

Obviously, Mike couldn't avoid a direct request. "Katie and me," he said, using the same name he'd given Clint.

"Okay, but while you're here, could you possibly take a look at one of the dogs in the clinic? She's not eating, and we're worried about her."

"Of course," Mike said, and gave Kat a questioning glance.

"How long do you think it will take?" Kat gestured toward the door, reminding Mike that Lira was still in the car.

"We won't be long," he promised.

Kat hesitated. She wasn't sure she wanted to leave Amber alone with Mike, but she didn't want to play tagalong either. "I'll just stay here and play with Scooter." Then, remembering what Mike had said earlier, she added, "Unless I could help in the socialization area?"

Amber gave Mike an uncertain look. "Many of our dogs have only had bad experiences with people and aren't as friendly as Scooter here."

"I understand that," Kat said.

"Ka—Katie would be perfect for that," Mike told Amber. "She's worked with animals all her life."

Amber smiled. "All right then. Follow me." She led them to the back of the building that was separated from the rest. "Here they are. Don't expect too much."

"I won't," Kat assured her. She glanced at the large, chain-link cages where most of the dogs cringed away from the three humans. "Who needs the most help?"

Amber crouched down next to a cage where an adorable fawn-colored Chihuahua tucked himself in the far corner and growled at them. "This little guy here—Samson. But he might be a bit much for your first time."

The poor little guy—he looked terrified. "I'll give it a shot," Kat said. When Amber looked doubtful, she added, "If I don't have any luck, I'll try another one. Don't worry—if I'm bitten, I won't blame you."

Amber shrugged as if to say, "It's your funeral," then grabbed Mike's arm again and pulled him away.

Eager for a distraction from the sight of Amber's hold on Mike, Kat stared down at the mighty little Samson, considering. Thankfully, she had a jacket pocket full of the treats Lira loved. Softly, she opened the door and entered the caged area with him. He continued to growl, and she sat down near him, but not too close. She spoke softly, soothingly. "It's okay, little guy. I won't do anything you don't like."

She scooted as close as she dared, carefully not looking him straight in the eyes, and hummed a lullaby. Then, slowly, carefully, she withdrew one of the small training treats and placed it halfway toward Samson.

He sniffed in its general direction, and obviously wanted it, but wasn't sure she was to be trusted. It didn't take long before he lunged for it and snatched it up, keeping a close eye on her the whole time.

Kat kept feeding him treats, one little piece at a time, until he seemed to trust her more. He moved a little closer and stopped growling. Encouraged, she kept on humming and slid her hand along the floor with a treat until he took it from her palm. A couple of treats later, he even allowed her to scratch under his chin.

He still looked as though he was going to bolt at any moment, but she felt certain that, with enough love and patience, he would be adoptable.

But they were both startled when a voice came from behind Kat. "Wow, you're quite the dog whisperer, aren't you?" Amber said in wonder as Samson dashed back to the safety of his corner.

Well, she was, until Amber scared the poor dog again.

"Told ya," Mike said with a grin, as if he knew this would happen. Then, to Kat, "Sorry we took so long."

"Did you?" She'd been so focused on Samson, she hadn't realized how much time had passed.

"It's been forty-five minutes, but I'm ready to go now."

"Okay." Kat got up stiffly from the hard floor. "He's a sweetie. He just needs someone to love him."

Amber beamed at her, as if she'd said the right thing. "They all do. Some more than others. And you're welcome back here anytime!"

"Thanks," Kat said. "I wish I could spend a lot of time here, but . . ." *I might be spending time in the prison on the outskirts of this town instead.*

"She lives in Denver," Mike explained as they moved out of the socialization area.

Amber took that cheerfully. "Well, the invitation still stands. And if we could lure you out to live here permanently, Mike, maybe Katie would be able to visit?"

That was well done—ask Mike to live close *and* make another subtle query about Kat's status at the same time. But Kat had to laugh. "Mike will never move," she

133

declared. "He still lives in the same house he grew up in."

"I might move," he said defensively. "Someday."

"Good," Amber declared. "We'd love to have you."

I bet you would. But Kat had to admit Amber was really likeable. The only question was, how much did *Mike* like her?

As the two of them headed toward the car, Kat had to ask. "So is there a . . . thing between the two of you?"

He looked surprised. "With Amber? No—she's like that with everyone. We're friends, nothing more."

Uh-huh. That may be what he thought, but it was obvious Amber wanted more. Kat decided not to enlighten him, though, and spent her time greeting an enthusiastic Lira, who had obviously been bored.

She let the dog out to pee and play for a little while. "So, what now?" she asked with resignation. She should be getting used to all these delays, and, to tell the truth, she didn't mind the necessity of spending more time with Mike. And *she* wouldn't cling like a limpet, unlike another person she could name.

"There's a bed and breakfast in town that takes dogs— Lavender Cottage." Mike grinned. "Then again, most of the places here in Dogwood accept animals."

"Sounds good." Better than the impersonal hotel room they'd stayed in the night before last.

Lavender Cottage certainly lived up to its name. Done in soft shades of lavender and cream, the Victorian house had an undeniable charm. She bet the owners probably grew lavender somewhere as well, though it was difficult to tell at this time of year.

"It's lovely," Kat exclaimed.

"I thought you'd like it. It won't take long to see if she has a room."

"She?"

"The owner—Betsy Mae Blake."

"Okay, but I'm coming in with you." She had to see inside this place. "Lira will be okay for a little while longer."

As tinkling bells announced their entrance, she realized the inside was as charming as the outside. Decorated with an odd combination of Victorian elegant fussiness and New Age crystals, it shouldn't have worked, but it did.

An older woman came in from the other room. Tall, slender, with beautiful white hair, she floated in with a swirl of chiffon skirts and trailing scarves. "Dr. Duffy," she exclaimed. "It's so nice to see you again." Her voice held a question.

"I'm sorry, Betsy Mae. I didn't know I was going to be needing a place to stay or I would have called you earlier. Do you have a room with two double beds plus accommodations for a dog?"

We'll be sharing a room again? Something thrilled through Kat. She told herself it was alarm, not anticipation, but it was Mike's money, and she wasn't about to tell him how to spend it.

"Of course. What kind of dog?"

"A . . . Bouvier mix," Mike lied. "She's well-behaved."

"And for how long?"

He gave Kat an uncertain glance. "I'm not sure yet."

"No problem," Betsy Mae said.

She showed them to a lovely room painted in navy and cream stripes, with coordinating damask bedspreads and curtains. Wedgwood blue accents here and there completed the elegant, somewhat less fussy look. There was even a large dog bed with matching food bowls in one corner. Kat definitely approved.

"Thank you," Mike said as he accepted the key.

"Did you need to walk your dog first?" Betsy Mae asked.

"Yes, good idea," Mike answered for Kat. "Why don't you do that while I unload the car?"

Betsy Mae nodded. "Go ahead and bring your dog through here, and I'll show you where the dog-walking area is."

Kat didn't know how to say no without being rude, so she brought Lira into the parlor while Mike grabbed their stuff. "This is Bruiser," she said firmly. "He's very well behaved."

"What a lovely boy," Betsy Mae said as she gave Lira a scrub on the ears. "Does he get along well with other dogs?"

"Yes, very well."

"Then I'll let my two out in the back with him and they can get acquainted."

She led Kat to the back of the house, and showed her the fenced-in area. "There are no other canine guests, so you can let Bruiser off the leash if you want."

Kat nodded and unclipped Lira's leash. Ecstatic to be released from confinement, Lira charged around the perimeter of the fence, then happily romped with Betsy Mae's two shih tzus.

After Lira was played out and Kat had wiped her wet feet, she made her way back to the room. With nothing to do but wait until tomorrow for the McPhersons to return home, Kat took off the hot wig and spent some time brushing Lira's unruly hair, then let the dog lie down in her own bed.

As Kat flopped on the bed, Mike grinned at her. "You know, you really are good with dogs—"

A knock at the door interrupted him, and he turned to open it.

Kat clutched at her wigless head and lunged up off the bed. "No, wait!"

But it was too late. He'd already opened the door to Betsy Mae and a man in uniform. The woman glanced at Kat, then at the dog, then at Mike. "That's Lira, isn't it?"

Oh, no! Not knowing what else to do, Kat slammed the door in her face.

CHAPTER FIFTEEN

MIKE STARED open-mouthed as annoyance surged through him. He closed his eyes and counted to ten. When he opened them, he reflected wryly that only Kat was able to make him lose his equanimity like this. "Give us a moment," he called to Betsy Mae.

Kat frantically ran around, gathering their things together. "Come on," she urged. "We have to get out of here!"

"No."

His simple, flat negative obviously got through to her, because she stopped and stared at him. "What?"

"No, you are not going to run away from your problems yet again."

"It's not running away if they really are chasing you."

That didn't make a whole lot of sense, but she continued cramming things in the duffel bag as if it did. How could he get through to her? When she struggled to open a window, he realized there was only one thing to do. He walked over and enveloped her in a confining hug. "Stop, please. This won't solve anything."

Her brow furrowed, Kat looked up at him pleadingly. "Yes, it will."

"Think. What's the most important thing right now?"

"To keep Lira safe."

"This is Dogwood, where animals are treated better than humans and cared for by everyone. Trust me—she's safer here than she would be anywhere else."

He felt her sag in his arms. "Well, maybe she is, but I'm not. Did you see the way Betsy Mae looked at me?"

"Like she thinks you stole a dog from its rightful owner? Who wouldn't, if they didn't know the whole story?"

"But—"

"But she doesn't know *why* you did it. And she won't unless you tell her."

As if on cue, another knock came at the door.

Mike squeezed her tighter. "Come on, it'll be all right. I'll keep you safe." He made his assurances sound more positive than he actually felt. He knew the people in this town, knew how they felt about animals—dogs, especially—and they knew him, respected him. It *should* be all right.

"Okay," Kat said in resignation, and pulled away from his hold to droop onto the bed.

He hated to see her so dejected, but this was the right thing to do. He opened the door. "Sorry about that," he told Betsy Mae and the officer beside her.

Lira bounded over to greet Betsy Mae, who she obviously saw as a friend. The B&B owner regarded Mike with a half-smile. "From your reactions, I'm guessing I was right," she drawled. "That *is* Lira, and your friend kidnapped her."

"It's not what you think," Kat protested.

"It's really not," Mike confirmed.

Betsy Mae cocked her head at them encouragingly. "Maybe Chief McPherson can help you sort it out."

"McPherson? Any relation to Paul and Sandy?" Mike asked as he shook the man's hand.

The man with the salt and pepper beard smiled genially. "Cousins of a sort. The McPhersons and Blakes founded this town, so you'll see a lot of those names here."

Mike relaxed a little, especially since the man didn't reach for his gun or handcuffs.

"Care to tell us about it, son?" the chief asked.

"Yes, I—" Then, noticing several people had opened doors down the hallway and were peering out curiously, Mike said, "Inside, if you don't mind."

The chief came inside and Betsy Mae followed him, evidently determined to hear the story for herself.

As Betsy Mae and the chief took the two chairs, Kat slumped on the bed with Lira, and Mike joined them, putting a reassuring hand on Kat's.

"How'd you know?" Kat asked Betsy Mae.

"I know my breeds, and while you might get away with convincing someone else that she's a Bouvier mix, I knew she was an Old English sheepdog immediately. Plus, when I scratched her ears, I noticed some places where half the hair shaft was white, and the other black. She was obviously dyed." She shrugged. "And I've been watching the reports about the movie star dog being stolen, so it was easy to put two and two together."

Kat lifted her chin. "I'm not a thief. I took her for her own protection."

"Tell us about it," the chief suggested. Thankfully, he wasn't one of those officious oafs some power-hungry public officials became. He was polite, genial, and set Kat at ease.

Mike let Kat tell the story her way, which included lots of hand-waving, dramatic language, and defensive explanations.

When she was done, the chief looked at Mike. "Can you corroborate this?"

"Yes." Well, minus the exaggerations. "At least, the parts I was involved in. And my assistant Aimee is the one who overheard Joey promise to kill Lira to collect the insurance. She has no reason to lie."

"Well, we certainly won't let him do that here," the chief promised.

"*Thank you,*" Kat said fervently.

"But there's a problem—the dog legally belongs to him."

"Not to him," Kat protested. "Lira belongs to his uncle, Edward Barton."

"Then, though Dogwood has ordinances in effect to protect Lira, it would be superseded by the state, who would insist Ms. Channing turn the dog over to Mr. Barton, her legal owner."

Oh, hell, he'd told Kat wrong, but he hadn't realized the full legal ramifications. Would Sanctuary be forced to give Lira up?

The chief continued, "And, once he removes her from Dogwood, there's nothing we can do."

"Even if he'll kill her?" Kat asked plaintively.

The chief paused, then said, "You said Mr. Barton didn't specifically tell his nephew to kill her for the insurance."

"No, but I know that's how Joey took it."

"Then perhaps Mr. Barton will be reasonable, and would just like to get Lira back. Have you tried asking him?"

"We tried to call him," Mike answered, "but he was unreachable for a few days."

"He might be back by now," Kat admitted, "but I lost his number with my phone, and he's unlisted, plus the studio won't give out his number to anyone."

"I'm sure they will to me," the chief said firmly. Oddly, his confidence seemed to reassure Kat. "Come with me down to the station," he suggested. "You can give me all the information, and I'll call him."

"Okay," Kat said reluctantly. "I just want to keep Lira safe."

"No problem," the chief assured her. "I'll ensure he knows that Dogwood will tell the world of his nephew's intentions, and, if he harms Lira, he'll never get the insurance."

Betsy Mae nodded with satisfaction. "And he'd probably never get another animal-handling job either."

Glad Kat was finally seeing sense and getting on board, Mike escorted her to the police car where he sat in front while Kat and Lira sat in back. Though Betsy Mae offered to watch the dog, Kat wasn't willing to let Lira out of her sight. Unfortunately, being locked in the back of a police car seemed to wear away at Kat's reasonableness, and, when they got to the station in the town square, the cold, impersonal look of the room the chief had them wait in seemed even more demoralizing. Lira took it in stride, flopping down to take a nap, but Kat was wound up again.

She glanced around the room with trepidation. "Is this an interrogation room?"

"Maybe. I don't know. Does it matter?"

"It does if they're going to interrogate us." She got up to test the doorknob. "It's locked," she said, her eyes wide.

"It's probably automatic," he soothed. "You've watched too many movies. Come on, sit down. Everything will be fine." At least, he hoped it would. Her nervousness was contagious. To calm himself as much as her, he grabbed her hand and pulled her down to the chair.

Kat grabbed onto it as if to a lifeline, steadying them both. "I've got you," Mike whispered.

Kat sighed. "I know. It's just . . . everything is so up in the air."

"Come here." Mike drew her into a gentle hug and kissed

her on the forehead. He wanted to keep her like this forever —safe and sound in his arms.

Kat snuggled closer, then lifted her head. "Thank you, Mike, for everything." Then she kissed him.

It was a light, quick kiss, probably intended to be a simple thank-you peck, but it slammed through his senses, awakening every nerve ending, just like the first one. Kat stared at him in wonder, her lips slightly parted, and he couldn't resist —he returned her kiss.

He poured a lifetime's worth of longing and love into that meeting of their lips, letting her know wordlessly just how much he cared for her. Kat's breath caught in her throat and she leaned into it, giving as good as she got.

Surprise and yearning thrilled through him. This was *so* not the right place or time . . . but it was definitely the right woman.

Kat laid a hand on his cheek and pulled away slightly, wonder in her eyes. "Mike, I—"

But the door opened then, so he didn't get to hear what she was going to say. Cursing the chief's timing, Mike turned to question the man with his eyes.

He looked apologetic, but said, "I have Mr. Barton on the line. I thought you might like to hear what he has to say."

"I would," Kat said eagerly, and followed the man down the hall into his office.

They all took seats, and the chief spoke into the phone. "I'll put you on speaker, Mr. Barton. I have Ms. Channing and Dr. Duffy in the office with me. Please, tell them what you told me."

"Kat," Edward said, "I assure you, I have no intentions of hurting Lira. That conversation you overhead—I was asking Joey to look for loopholes in the insurance policy, to see if she could be covered for her blindness. I didn't intend for him to *kill* her."

That was a relief, and exactly what Mike had assumed.

"That's not how he took it," Kat said indignantly.

"I know that now—his message made that very clear. Is Lira safe?"

"She's safe here," Mike replied for her, reassured by Edward's concern for the dog. "But will you please call Joey off?"

"I would, but he's unreachable. He must have turned his phone off or something, because he's not answering."

Mike wondered idly if it had gone the same way Kat's phone had.

"Why would he do that?" the chief asked.

"He's totally paranoid about GPS on phones," Edward said, sounding annoyed. "He's probably worried Kat could track him that way."

Kat rolled her eyes. "As if I would know how to do that. And Lira's still in danger."

Mike sighed. Damn it. They were back where they started, with no way to find the self-appointed hit man who had Lira in his sights.

CHAPTER SIXTEEN

"What can we do now?" Kat asked, trying not to wail.

"Nothing we can do," the chief said, "except keep an eye out for him and intercept him. Will he know where you are?"

"How could he?" Kat exclaimed.

"I'll come pick up Lira," Edward declared. "And I'll tell him to stop."

"How can you, if you can't reach him?" Kat asked.

"Mr. Barton," the police chief said sternly, "I don't want to release the dog to you unless we're certain she won't be injured."

"You can't do that. The dog is my property. I'll sue."

Chief McPherson frowned at that—more at the "property" comment than the threat to sue, Kat figured approvingly.

Mike jumped in. "And then the story will come out that you wanted Lira dead to collect the insurance money."

"But I didn't!"

"Public opinion may not see it that way," Mike said reasonably.

Kat mouthed "thank you" to Mike. She wouldn't have thought of that. He gave her a reassuring smile.

"So, what do you suggest?" Edward asked belligerently.

"I have an idea," Mike said, "if the chief is okay with it. Why don't we plant a story saying she's been spotted here at Sanctuary? That should bring Joey here."

"Do we want him here?" Kat asked, leaning down to scratch Lira's ears.

The chief nodded. "If we can get Sanctuary to agree, we can keep an eye out for his car and protect Lira." He turned to address the phone again. "Mr. Barton, do you have a picture of your nephew, and can you tell us what kind of car he's driving?"

"Yes to both of those. But I'm coming anyway. I need to tell my nephew a thing or two."

Well, at least he'd transferred his anger to Joey instead of her, Kat mused.

"Can you recommend a place to stay?" Edward asked.

"The Harrington," Mike put in quickly.

The chief gave him an odd look, but nodded. "Please check in with me when you get to town, Mr. Barton."

"Oh, I will."

Edward hung up and Kat asked, "The Harrington?"

"They don't allow dogs," Mike explained. "Not even movie stars. The owner's allergic."

"Oh, good." Mike was always looking after her . . . and Lira.

"Paul and Sandy are out of town," Mike explained to the chief, "and won't be back until tomorrow. But we plan on going out there as soon as they're back. I'll ask them then."

"All right, son. Keep me posted."

Kat hesitated, hoping. "Does that mean I'm not under arrest?"

"Not yet," the chief clarified. "But if Mr. Barton presses charges . . ."

Well, crap. Edward could be vindictive.

Mike squeezed her hand. "If he tries it, I'll threaten to tell the whole truth to the world."

"Thanks, Mike, but I couldn't ask you to risk your career like that." What pet owners would trust a vet who'd aided and abetted a dognapper?

"It's my decision, not yours."

She let him think that, but wouldn't let him take the risk for her. Not again. It was the Rat Incident all over again. "Let's head back to the B&B."

They did, and Betsy Mae was happy to hear about the change in circumstances. They ate dinner, then ended up back in the bedroom where she was left all alone with Mike . . . and Lira, of course.

While in the police station, she'd been able to ignore the kiss they'd shared, but now that they were alone . . .

Not so much.

She didn't know what to do, what to say, and it seemed Mike didn't either. But he kept looking at her mouth, which made her want to squirm. That kiss . . . that kiss had meant everything to her. Too much, as a matter of fact.

She'd only meant to give him a quick peck on the lips, but her impulsiveness had cost her again, like always. His return kiss had made her feel cherished, safe, and filled a void she hadn't even known existed. Could it be that she was more than a little in love with the guy she'd known since they were kids?

No. This couldn't happen. She was bad for him. He'd said so, and she'd proved it time and again. But maybe . . .

For a moment, she let herself daydream about what life would be like with Mike. But only an instant. Because, she reminded herself, that's what her parents had thought too, and look what had happened to them. They'd ended up miserable and hating each other in the end. She couldn't lose Mike as a friend. She just couldn't.

Mike cocked his head at her. "Do you want to talk—"

"No." She suspected he wanted to talk about that kiss, and she wasn't ready for that at all. "I just want to read." She picked up one of the books Betsy Mae had left in the room. "I've been wanting to read this one."

"Okay," Mike said doubtfully.

Kat curled up on one of the beds with her back to Mike and pretended to read. Soon, she realized she probably should have chosen one less at random. This gritty murder mystery wasn't really her thing. It didn't hold her attention, either, and she fell asleep, and didn't wake until the morning when she heard the door open. She jerked awake, and blearily spotted Mike coming in with Lira on a leash.

"I fed and walked her for you," he said. "Ready for breakfast? Betsy Mae has a huge spread."

She rubbed the sleep from her eyes and murmured, "Let me take a quick shower and change clothes."

When she emerged, Mike said, "Look, Kat. I'm sorry about the kiss—"

She cut him off. "Nothing to apologize for." She didn't want to hear that he was sorry about kissing her. Not when it had affected her so profoundly. "My fault. I don't want to talk about it."

"But—"

"I mean it, Mike. Let's go for breakfast."

After they ate, they headed toward Sanctuary by mutual consent. Kat didn't really want to be alone with Mike, and he seemed just as uncomfortable. Maybe even disappointed? Kat wasn't sure, but it wasn't something she wanted to explore. If they were around other people, it would be a heck of a lot easier to ignore this chemistry between them.

She'd decided to leave the wig off, since the cat was out of the bag—or, rather, the dog. When they arrived at Sanctuary, Amber glanced at her blond curls curiously. "I wore a wig yesterday," Kat said, not bothering to explain why, choosing to let Amber come up with any explanation she chose.

"I heard from Mom and Dad this morning," Amber told them, taking Mike's arm again. "They should be here in an hour or so. Want to take a look at some of our patients in the clinic?"

"Sure," Mike said, and glanced at Kat questioningly.

Feeling distinctly like a fifth wheel, Kat said, "I'll spend some more time in the socialization area, if that's okay."

"Of course."

"Can I bring my dog in?" Kat gestured toward Lira, who was peering at them through the window. "She's well-behaved."

Amber glanced doubtfully at Mike, but when gave her a nod, she said, "Okay. I don't have to tell you to be careful with her around the other dogs."

"That's right." *You don't.*

As Amber dragged Mike away, Kat went back out to visit Samson. Lira actually helped the little dog since he felt safe around her.

Feeling good about Samson, she spread her time amongst some of the other dogs. She felt so bad for them, and wanted to do something—anything—to help. Besides, they helped keep her mind off her uncertain future. Being in limbo was no fun.

She was relieved when a teenage boy came to fetch her. The volunteer led her to an open area in the back where Mike, Amber, and an older couple were waiting for them. The man was tall and distinguished-looking even in jeans and a casual shirt, with dark hair lightly dusted with gray, and the woman had hair the same golden blond as Amber's.

She was dressed casually as well—a necessity when dealing with this many animals. They must be Paul and Sandy—Amber's parents.

Sandy glanced up when she saw the volunteer and Kat in the doorway. "Thank you, Jesse." Then, to Kat, "You must be Mike's friend. Come on in."

As Jesse left, Kat glanced around curiously. The open area had a number of dog beds and couches. What did they use this for?

As if she'd read her mind, Sandy said, "This is where we let prospective parents meet the dogs, and where they wait while the dogs come out of surgery." She nodded toward Mike. "Where generous vets like Mike neuter the dogs."

Amber patted Mike's arm. "He was so helpful in the clinic," she exclaimed to her parents. "He has such a way with them, we need him here permanently."

Paul shook his head. "He can't do pro bono work all the time. He does need to make a living, you know." Turning to Kat, he held out his hand. "I'm Paul McPherson, and this is my wife, Sandy."

Kat shook his hand, but was at a loss for how to introduce herself. She glanced at Mike, who gave her an encouraging nod. Time for the truth. "I'm Kat Channing. Mike and I were next-door neighbors growing up."

Amber gave her a sharp glance, but didn't say anything.

"Please, take a seat," Paul said.

Kat released Lira, who bounded over to a bed in the corner as Kat sank onto a couch next to Mike. She wasn't looking forward to this, and needed Mike's support.

Mike squeezed her hand. "Did you want to . . . ?"

She shook her head. "Will you?" She'd probably stumble over the words and look even more guilty than she really was. Besides, these people liked and trusted Mike—it would sound better coming from him.

"Of course." He turned to Paul and Sandy, who sat together, holding hands, on another couch. "Have you heard reports on the news about Lira, the movie star dog, going missing?"

They nodded, and Mike added, "Well, that's Lira." He nodded toward the sheepdog.

The three McPhersons turned to stare at Lira who lay happily in the bed in the corner, chewing on a rope.

"But she's—" Sandy stopped herself. "Oh, I see. You've dyed her hair."

"Yes," Mike said smoothly.

"You *kidnapped* a famous dog?" Amber asked incredulously.

"He didn't," Kat said defensively. "I did."

"*Why?*"

Kat looked pleadingly at Mike, and he picked up the tale. "Because Lira's life was in danger. Edward Barton is Lira's trainer, and Kat is his assistant. Lira is losing her eyesight, which means she'll no longer be able to work, and his nephew, Joey, thinks his uncle wants him to kill the dog to collect the insurance on her. Kat overheard and brought her to me to keep her safe."

Well, that was certainly more succinct than she'd been in explaining it to Chief McPherson yesterday.

Amber speared her with a disgusted look. "You involved Mike in your crime? How could you jeopardize his career like that? And us?"

Kat felt her cheeks flush with heat, but before she could defend herself, Paul chided, "Amber, let them explain."

Mike said, "We've explained it all to Lira's trainer and to Chief McPherson and we have a plan to stop Joey and save Lira, but we need your help." He went on to explain more about how all this had come about, and ended with, "So, if you're willing, I'd like to put the word out that Sanctuary has taken Lira in, so we can draw Joey out, and his uncle can talk some sense into him."

"That sounds dangerous," Amber exclaimed.

"Not really," Mike said. "The chief has agreed to provide protection, if you agree to help."

Paul and Sandy exchanged a glance, and seemed to communicate wordlessly. "What do you need us to do?" Paul asked.

Good question. Kat wondered what Mike had in mind as well.

"You can't be serious," Amber said, actually moving away from Mike for once.

"Would you rather we let this Joey kill the dog?" Sandy asked her daughter.

"No, but—"

"This is what Sanctuary is for," Paul said gently. Then, to Mike, he added, "So long as we don't put any of the other animals in jeopardy."

"No one else should be in danger," Mike said. "Joey is only after Lira. He thinks he's helping his uncle." He hesitated. "We don't actually need to keep Lira here. I mainly want your permission to say Lira is safe at Sanctuary."

"You have it," Paul said.

"Good. Edward should be here some time today. Let me talk to him and the chief and we'll come up with a plan to waylay Joey before he has a chance to harm Lira."

"Sounds good," Paul said. Both men rose and shook hands, and the women rose as well.

"Be careful," Amber told Mike as she shot a warning glance at Kat.

Obviously, the woman had placed all the blame for this situation directly on Kat.

Well, who could blame her? Kat wasn't responsible for putting Lira in danger, but she had to admit she didn't know what Joey would do if someone tried to stop him. She'd put Mike, Betsy Mae, the McPhersons, and everyone else in town in danger.

As Kat and Mike drove away from Sanctuary with Lira in the back seat once more, Mike got a phone call from the police station, letting him know Edward had arrived. He glanced at Kat. "Are you worried about seeing Edward again?"

She shrugged. "Kind of. I'm more afraid that he'll insist on taking Lira, and that the chief will let him."

Mike thought for a moment. "How about I drop you and Lira off at Lavender Cottage? I'll meet the chief and Edward at the station, and the three of us can make a plan to stop Joey."

"Okay," Kat said listlessly, feeling like a total screw-up.

He dropped them off at the B&B, saying, "Everything will be okay. I promise."

Kat nodded and took Lira inside. She believed he meant well, but he couldn't promise that Joey would be reasonable, that he wouldn't harm anyone . . . that Kat wouldn't mess everything up again.

Sighing, she sat on the bed and rubbed the playful dog's belly. "I love you, sweetie," she said, leaning down to kiss her head. When Lira nosed her to continue with the belly rubs, Kat complied. "You won't get this from Edward, you know. He disapproves of 'coddling' animals."

Lira sighed happily, and Kat shook her head. "Even if we do stop Joey, what will happen to you? Will you have to go back to Edward?" To a life devoid of affection? Without someone to love the dog as she deserved? Lira deserved retirement after a lifetime of hard work.

Kat would love to keep Lira as her own, but with no job, no place to live, and no prospects, it might be a tad difficult.

"I'll find a good home for you, I promise. Though I really wish I could keep you with me forever."

The sweet dog licked her hand as if to say she wanted that, too. Unfortunately, the law might put a kibosh on any plans Kat came up with. Unless . . . maybe Mike had the right idea, using the court of public opinion. It certainly mattered to Edward. If she got the word out about how bleak Lira's life really was, the dog's legion of fans would certainly be on Kat's side.

But then Kat's own actions would come out in the process. She was willing to take the heat for what she'd done to help Lira . . . but what about Mike? Would Mike lose his job or his patients once the story came out?

"None of this is his fault," Kat murmured as she continued to stroke the dog. "And I can't let his career suffer because of me."

But how could she keep that from happening? Especially when Mike had just involved himself even more? Kat sighed. There was only one thing to do—she had to distance herself from Mike, tell the story the way she wanted it told, and leave Mike out of it altogether.

Tears threatened as she thought about living without her best friend again. Okay, yeah, she had to admit they were becoming more than friends . . . and that she loved the new, mature, sexier man he'd become. Oh, sure, she'd always loved him, but as her best friend. Now, however, she was afraid she'd fallen in love with him.

Who wouldn't? He was kind, nice, funny . . . and looked mighty good with his shirt off.

She shook her head to wipe the image away.

All that was irrelevant. He was better off without her. She blinked back the tears as she reminded herself that he deserved someone who would love him and not get him into stupid, crazy situations. Someone like Amber.

She grimaced at the thought, but the two were perfect for each other. They shared an interest in animals, both worked with Sanctuary, and Amber obviously adored him. She'd be good for him—much better than Kat.

So, for his sake—and Lira's—there was only one thing she could do.

After she made a quick phone call, she said, "Come on, girl. Let's blow this popsicle stand."

CHAPTER SEVENTEEN

"So, we have a plan," Mike said to the chief and Barton. A lot of things were unknown, of course, since they couldn't predict when Joey would arrive in Dogwood, or what he'd do when he got here, but they'd tried to cover all contingencies. And since both men were concerned about Lira's fate, Mike was satisfied they'd do what was in the dog's best interest.

But he wasn't so sure about Kat's. He glanced at Barton. "You know Kat was only trying to save Lira."

Barton grimaced. "Yeah, I know. But she should have talked to me first."

"Well, at first, she thought you told Joey to kill Lira for the insurance," Mike reminded him.

Barton rolled his eyes. "That's the problem—she doesn't think."

"She is impulsive at times," Mike conceded, "but she means well, and her primary concern is always the animals' welfare." He paused, and then, encouraged by Barton's thoughtful expression, said, "So you won't press charges?" He didn't want to remind the man of the threat to broadcast the whole story, but Barton remembered, if the sour look on his face was any indication.

"No, I won't press charges. Not if I get Lira back." Before Mike could ask for more, Barton raised his hands in surrender. "And I'll announce publicly that it was a mistake, that Lira wasn't kidnapped, just brought here for a rest because of her failing eyesight." He sighed. "The word about her disease will get out, anyway."

"So you'll let Lira retire?" the chief asked.

"I guess I'll have to—she can't see anymore, but she can still do public appearances. Especially to promote the movie."

Mike would have to accept that. "And will you give Kat back her job?"

Barton scowled. "Not a chance."

Guess I pushed it too far. No matter—he'd take care of Kat and help her land on her feet.

Satisfied he'd done what he could to help Kat and Lira, Mike headed back to the B&B. When he entered, he found Betsy Mae in the foyer.

She waved a piece of paper at him. "I have a note for you, Dr. Duffy."

"For me?"

"Yes, your friend left it."

What friend? Who knew he was here besides Kat?

Oh, no. She didn't. . . . Mike took the note and read it with a feeling of dread.

Dear Mike,

I'm so sorry for involving you in my problems again, but I'll make sure your job isn't in jeopardy. Don't worry about me—I'll be fine.

Take care,

Kat

Mike swore and crumpled the note in his hand. Crap.

He'd finally figured everything out, and she had to run off again.

Betsy Mae raised her eyebrows, then noted, "She's left, hasn't she?"

Mike resisted the urge to roll his eyes. Of course—that's what Kat did. But he answered simply, "Yes."

"Did she say why?"

He shook his head. "She's trying to protect me, keep me from losing my license." Little did she know that it meant nothing if it meant he didn't have Kat. He started to thrust his hand through his hair, aborted the gesture, then realized Lira wasn't there to howl.

"That seems like a good reason," Betsy Mae said slowly. "Why are you upset?"

"I'm not upset—I'm frustrated."

"Okay," she said doubtfully. "But do you want to get her back?"

"Of course I do! We just came up with a plan to fix everything."

"I'm glad to hear it, but may I make an observation?"

Could he stop her? He nodded.

"You've stayed here a lot over the past few years, and I've never seen you lose your cool, never seen you so distracted."

He grimaced. "Kat would try the patience of a saint." *And I'm no saint.*

Betsy Mae smiled. "She's good for you."

"Huh?" How did that follow?

"You're not so uptight, controlled. I've seen more of the real you on this trip than I have any other. And I like what I see. She brings you out of your safe little cave. It's good for you."

"I'll let her know you think so," Mike said dryly. "If I can find her. Did she say or hint at where she was going?"

"Sorry, no. But when you do find her, let her know you care for her."

"What?" She was giving him whiplash with all these conversational changes.

"It's obvious you love her—tell her so."

Of course he loved her. He'd loved her all his life. But . . . "She doesn't want to hear it. I'm not her type." Especially since she wouldn't even talk about the kiss.

"Actually, you're wrong on both counts."

Mike didn't have the time to argue with her or explain their shared past. "Sorry, gotta go. I'll drive around, see if I can find her."

Betsy Mae nodded. "And I'll call some people, see if anyone has seen her. I have a lot of contacts in town."

"Thank you. You'll call if you hear something?"

"Of course." And, as Mike rushed out the door, she called after him, "Think about what I said."

No time. The important thing was to find Kat. She didn't have a car, had limited cash, and a big sheepdog to hide. Where could she have gone? And what the hell was she thinking, anyway?

Oh, yeah, this was Kat. She didn't think—she just acted.

As he drove, he spotted an older man out walking his dachshund. "Excuse me," Mike called. "But have you seen a woman with a dog?"

The man gave him an odd look. "This is Dogwood. There are lots of dogs . . . but not enough women, if you ask me." He slapped his knee and cackled, as if it was the funniest joke in the world.

Of course—dog walking wasn't exactly a strange sight here. Mike shook his head in exasperation, then described Kat and Lira.

"Nope. Sorry, haven't seen them."

Mike drove on, getting increasingly more frustrated as there was no sign of Kat or Lira. This was getting him nowhere. Wherever Kat was, he hoped she was safe, warm, and staying out of trouble.

But he couldn't give up. Kat had been abandoned—emotionally if not physically—by her parents and every boyfriend she'd gotten close to. He was *not* going to be added to that list. She didn't know it yet, but he would always be there for her, always help her out of her scrapes.

He just had to find her first. But how?

Well, there was one thing he could think of. It was chancy, but he had to try it. Quickly, he called Chief McPherson. "There's been a slight change of plans. Here's what I'd like to do."

❦ ❦ ❦ ❦

AFTER KAT PACKED her things and Lira's, and got something to eat at the nearby dog-friendly Blossom Café, her walk to her appointment was only a few blocks. But with the bite in the air, carrying the duffel bag, and worrying about Lira being spotted, it seemed much longer.

"Welcome to KDGW Radio," the brunette at the reception desk said, giving her an uncertain look.

Kat smiled at her, as if there was nothing wrong with arriving for a meeting, looking windblown with a huge dog and her luggage in tow. Glancing at the receptionist's name plate, she said, "Hi, Brittany. I called earlier and have an appointment to see . . . Mitch? The news guy."

Brittany's expression lightened. "Oh, yes. But, actually, our station manager, Tad Brightwell, would like to see you."

"Why?" Kat asked apprehensively.

"I don't know," Brittany said. "Not everyone gets to see

the big boss, but he's a really nice guy, so don't worry." She stood and gestured toward a hallway. "If you'll follow me?" She gave the duffel bag an odd look, but didn't seem too concerned about Lira, thank goodness.

Well, maybe this Mitch guy needed the boss's approval for this kind of thing. Kat followed her down the hall, and Brittany stuck her head in an office. "Tad? That lady you wanted to see is here."

Hmm, if he allowed his employees to call him by his first name, he couldn't be too bad.

"Come on in," he said. Glancing at Brittany, he said, "You'll make that phone call?"

Brittany nodded and closed the door behind her. Tad, a tall, blond older man with a great smile, held out his hand in greeting.

She shook it. "Hi, I'm Kat . . . Kat Channing." No sense in lying now. Seeing him glance down at Lira, she gave the dog the cue to shake hands, and Lira raised her paw to Tad.

He shook it with a grin, and said, "Please, have a seat."

As she sat in one of the two visitor chairs, she noticed a golden retriever vegging out in the corner of the office. Ah, that explained why Brittany wasn't concerned about Lira. The two dogs sniffed each other, but the golden—an old girl by the looks of her—didn't even move from her bed.

Tad took a seat behind the desk as Lira flopped on the floor beside Kat. "So, Mitch said you have a story for us?" he asked.

"Yes, the real story about Lira, the famous movie star dog. This is Lira."

He didn't react, just continued to look affable. "Tell me about it."

Kat told him the whole story. Well, most of it anyway. She left out Mike's part in the kidnapping, and painted Joey and

Edward as the bad guys, which they totally deserved. The story took longer than she expected, because he kept asking questions. Good ones. She was careful to tell the truth . . . just not the *whole* truth.

"So, why do you want this story to come out?" Tad asked.

"So Joey won't hurt her, obviously." Kat scrubbed Lira's ears. "And I don't want her to go back to that kind of life afterward."

"What was wrong with it?"

"Well, she's well-fed and likes her job," she admitted. "And though she gets lots of attention when she's in public, they treat her as a commodity, not as a beloved companion. She deserves to be loved all the time."

"So what will you do if we air this story?"

This wasn't going at all like she expected. "What do you mean?"

"We care about dogs in this town. According to your own story, you have no job, no place to live, no car. How do you expect to take care of Lira?"

Okay, that did seem bad. She seized on the one item she could account for. "I do have a car—it's in Colorado Springs."

"How are you going to get to it? Hitchhike?"

Maybe. But she said, "I hadn't thought about it. I guess I'll take a taxi, or an Uber or something."

He smiled gently. "I take it you haven't thought about a lot of things. How will you take care of Lira after the story comes out, especially if her owner wants her back?"

She'd worry about that later. "Public opinion will be on my side . . . if you tell the story the right way."

"The public can be fickle. What if it goes against you? What if you have to turn Lira over to her owner?"

She raised her chin. "I won't let that happen."

"So you'll go into hiding? That's no life."

Okay, maybe she hadn't thought this through all that well, but her intentions were really good. "Well, I may not be able to take care of her myself, but I'll find someone who will love her and give her the life she deserves. Sanctuary will help, I'm sure." Before he could ask another question, she said, "Besides, I'm sure the public will see it the way I do. Will you air the story?"

He sat back in his chair and regarded her thoughtfully. "Before we air this story, we'd have to check it out, get corroboration. We don't want to be accused of irresponsible journalism."

She understood that, but had to protest. "But it's urgent. Joey wants to *kill* her." Didn't he realize the dog was in real danger?

Tad cocked his head and regarded her thoughtfully. "Have you told us the whole story?"

"Of course," she exclaimed, mentally crossing her fingers.

"What about the vet?"

Frantically, she wondered why he asked, then remembered the earlier radio report. "Oh, you mean the gray van? Those kids who reported it must have been drunk or wanted attention."

"No, I mean the veterinarian you stopped to see before you came to Dogwood."

How did he know that? She hadn't mentioned it. "Oh. Uh, I just wanted to get confirmation of Lira's diagnosis first. That's all."

"That's funny. That's not what he said."

"Wha-at? Who?"

"Dr. Duffy."

"Mike?" she repeated in a voice that sounded squeaky and guilty, even to her.

"Yes. He called here to tell us the story, but it differs from yours in a few respects."

Well, crap. Mike wouldn't even let her do this for him? Before she could ask for more information, Tad's phone buzzed. He answered it and said, "Yes, thanks. . . . Send him in."

Now what?

The door opened, and her mouth dropped open when she saw who was on the other side—Mike.

The dots connected—the phone call he'd told Brittany to make, his wanting to hear the whole story, but knowing parts she hadn't related . . .

She swiveled to glare at Tad. "You were stalling?"

He shrugged. "A little. But I wanted to hear your side of the story as well." He gave her a half smile. "It was the same as his . . . though you managed to leave him out of the narrative entirely."

She rolled her eyes. "That's because I don't want Mike mentioned in any of this at all. It might hurt his career."

"It's okay, Kat," Mike said.

"No, it's not." She glared at Tad again. "So, will you air the story without mentioning Mike? Chief McPherson knows all the details. No one else needs to."

The station manager sighed. "My main concern is the dog's welfare. You two talk it out, then let me know how I can help." He checked his watch. "I have a meeting now, so you can have this office to discuss it for the next half hour or so." With that, he left, taking his golden with him.

Instead of taking Tad's chair, Mike sat in the other visitor's chair next to Kat.

"I know, I know," she said with a sigh, not meeting his eyes. "I was impulsive, didn't think things through, and ran away again. Go ahead, say it."

"I don't have to," Mike said gently. "Kat, look at me."

She didn't want to, didn't want to see the disappointment

in his eyes, but he used one finger to raise her chin so she had to.

All she saw was compassion, maybe a little sadness. "I know you did it for a good reason," Mike continued. "You wanted to protect me, like you did after the Rat Incident."

"Yeah," Kat muttered.

"But I don't need you to . . . and I don't want you to, either."

She glanced sharply at him. "You don't?"

He smiled ruefully. "No man likes to feel as though a woman thinks she needs to protect him. It usually goes the other way."

"Well, that's just silly."

He shrugged. "But not untrue. Is that the only reason you ran?"

"What other reason would there be?"

"Did . . . our kiss have something to do with it?"

She felt her face warm, but couldn't reply. She lowered her eyes and pretended to be absorbed in petting Lira. She shook her head.

"You know I would never do anything you don't like," Mike said softly.

"But I did like it," she blurted, then immediately regretted her impulsive tongue.

He laughed, and he looked so wonderful when his eyes crinkled that way, the sight went straight to her heart.

"I'm no good for you," she whispered. "I'd ruin your life." It would never work.

"I don't agree," he said firmly, still smiling. "But this isn't the time to discuss that."

She didn't know if there would ever be a good time, but she nodded anyway. What was it they were supposed to talk about? Oh, yeah. Lira. "So, why did you call the radio station? To get the word out about Lira being at Sanctuary?"

"Yes, that, and I wanted them to ask Dogwood citizens to be on the lookout for you and call me if they spotted you." He smiled. "I wasn't about to let you get away so easily."

She couldn't help it—she melted. "Really?" she asked wistfully.

"That is, if you promise not to run away from me again."

Kat knew herself, and knew she couldn't promise that. She shrugged. "The only thing I'm concerned about right now is keeping Lira safe." And Mike, too, though she knew better than to say that out loud.

"We had the station announce earlier that Lira is at Sanctuary. With any luck, Joey will hear it and go there. We'll be ready for—"

Mike's cell rang. He answered it, and turned to smile at Kat. "Thanks," he said, and hung up. "Joey was spotted at the Blossom Café, asking for directions to Sanctuary. We need to go."

"But . . . the story."

"We'll figure it out later. With the directions the waitress gave him, it may be awhile before he gets there. Come on. We can beat him there."

Though the discussion was over for the moment, Kat was determined she wouldn't let him change her mind. He was *not* going to suffer for her mistakes.

When they arrived at Sanctuary, Kat glanced out the car window, seeking evidence of Lira's protection. "I don't see anyone," she said doubtfully.

"Well, if they're doing their job right, you shouldn't," Mike said, though he glanced around uncertainly as well. "Maybe they're hiding in the trees. You know, to keep a low profile so Joey doesn't spot them. Or maybe they're all inside—it's cold out here."

"Maybe," Kat said doubtfully. "What's your plan?"

"It's very simple. When Joey goes in to Sanctuary to look

for Lira, Edward can explain Joey's misunderstanding of the situation."

"What if Joey doesn't listen?"

"He wants to please his uncle, right?"

"Well, yeah, but—"

"Then there should be no problem. And if there is, Chief McPherson will do whatever needs to be done to stop him." He squeezed her hand. "It'll be okay. Let me go inside and see where the chief wants you and Lira." He shook his head as if annoyed with himself. "Oh, and I forgot to tell you— Edward agreed not to press charges against you *and* to let Lira retire."

Some of the tension left her body. "Thank you," she said fervently. Now that this ordeal was almost over, she spared a thought for the future and those very pertinent questions Tad had asked. "Mike, did you mean it when you said I could stay with you after this is over? Just until I find another job," she assured him.

"Of course. Stay as long as you like."

"Lira too?" If she was allowed to keep her.

"No question. What kind of vet would I be if I didn't like animals?" He quirked a smile at her, and started to exit the car, then paused. "But, Kat . . ."

"What?"

"You scared the heck out of me. Please, don't ever take off like that again without telling me first."

"Okay." She guessed she owed him that much. But what was that very odd expression on his face? "What's wrong?"

"Oh, what the hell," he muttered, and gave her a swift, hard kiss. "Stay safe," he said, then got out of the car and headed for the building.

"Oh, my," Kat breathed, her fingers to her lips. Maybe staying with him wouldn't be such a great idea after all. How would she be able to resist him?

Then again, it was either that or bunk with her mother or father. Neither of those choices appealed. . . .

Lira whined a little, wanting out, and Kat leaned into the back seat to pet the dog. "Shh, it shouldn't be much longer, girl."

But the dog continued to whine, and Kat realized she hadn't had a potty break in quite a while. "Okay, we'll go out for a little ways, but then we'll have to get back in the car."

She let Lira out, and the dog bounded to the trees where she immediately squatted. Kat glanced around, looking for any sign of police officers, and saw movement in the trees across the parking lot. She started to wave, then realized that was no police officer—that was Joey!

Worse, when he shifted position, she saw something glint in his hand. *Omigod, he has a gun!*

Kat ducked down behind the car and froze. Joey hadn't noticed them yet. She had to warn Mike—*before* he came outside again! But how? She still didn't have a phone. The car horn? No, that would draw Joey's attention to her and Lira.

Lira. . . .

If she moved, Joey would see her. Frantically, Kat tried to get the dog's attention to cue her to stay, but Lira was too busy sniffing everything in sight. Kat obviously couldn't call out to her either, to get her attention.

Crap, crap, crap.

The Sanctuary door opened and her heart leapt into her throat. *No . . .*

But it wasn't Mike—it was Edward, and it looked like he was headed for his car. Thank goodness—Joey wouldn't harm him. But when she glanced at Lira, she saw the huge dog barreling toward Edward, joy on her face at seeing her trainer.

"No," she screamed, rising to her feet and stretching her arms out. Yeah, right, as if that would stop anything.

Then everything happened at once. Joey brought the gun up to aim at Lira . . . Edward's head jerked up at Kat's yell, then he darted between Joey and Lira, yelling, "Stop!"

But it was too late. Joey's pistol bucked, and Edward went down.

Kat covered her mouth in horror. *Oh, no. What have I done?*

CHAPTER EIGHTEEN

JOEY STARED open-mouthed at his uncle on the ground, and, before he could raise his pistol again, Kat belatedly remembered Lira's training. She splayed out her hands toward him, and yelled, "Stop!"

As Edward had taught her, Lira responded immediately to the cue to protect Kat. She tackled Joey to the ground, baring her teeth at his throat.

Crap. I should have thought of this earlier. She wanted to run toward Edward, but had to keep an eye on Joey to make sure he didn't hurt anyone else.

"Call her off," Joey screamed. "It was an accident, I swear. I didn't mean to hurt him!"

"No way," Kat declared, running to kick the pistol away from Joey, who was lying with ninety pounds of menacing sheepdog on his chest.

Mike and several policemen came running out of Sanctuary. Mike rushed to her while the policemen moved to check on Edward and Joey. The Sanctuary employees rubbernecked, wide-eyed, from the protection of the building, where they wisely stayed out of the way.

Kat watched, her heart in her throat, as the men checked on Edward. If only Joey hadn't been so impulsive—

And then it hit her. Wasn't that what Mike had been accusing her of all along? She closed her eyes in sudden, sinking realization. This wasn't Joey's fault—it was hers for putting Edward in this situation. She couldn't blame Joey without blaming herself. This was all her fault.

As the enormity of what she'd done finally hit her, she froze in dismay.

Mike grabbed her by the shoulders and shook her. "Kat, call her off!"

Her eyes popped open. "Huh?"

"Get Lira off Joey—the police can take over now, but she won't let them. You have to call her off first."

"Oh, okay."

Kat gave Lira the cue to stand down, and the dog bounded over to nose her trainer as the police hauled Joey to his feet and cuffed him.

Kat peered over at Edward. "Is he . . . dead?"

"I don't know," Mike said, and put his arm around her to hold her, in an obvious attempt to comfort her. It didn't work. *Please, don't be dead. . . .*

"No," Joey shouted. "I didn't mean to shoot him! And I wasn't going to hurt Lira either. It's only a tranq gun, I swear!"

Chief McPherson pulled a dart from Edward's side. "Looks like he's telling the truth."

Oh, thank heavens. Kat's knees went rubbery with relief, but luckily, Mike was there to steady her, like always.

Edward sat up, holding a hand to his head. "You impulsive idiot," he yelled at Joey.

Kat winced, but Edward wasn't done. "I wanted you to look at the insurance docs, find a loophole, not off the dog, you moron."

Joey was dumbstruck for a moment, then finally said, "Oh. Well, I couldn't bring myself to kill her anyway. I was just going to tranq her, take her somewhere far away, and tell everyone she was dead."

"You—" Edward started to stand up, but didn't get very far. He shook his head and sat back down with a thump.

"Relax," the chief said, placing his hand on Edward's shoulder. "That tranquilizer may be taking effect, and we don't know the dosage or how it will affect you. An ambulance is on its way. We can sort it all out at the police station later."

Lira tried to lick her trainer's face in sympathy, but Edward pushed her away weakly.

The police chief turned to look at her. "Ms. Channing, will you take charge of Lira, please?"

So many emotions were flowing through Kat right now that she couldn't speak. She nodded, and gave Lira the cue to come. The cheerful dog complied, and Kat buried her face in Lira's welcoming fur. At last, they were safe.

"I'd like both of you to come to the police station as well," the chief added to Mike, "so we can sort this out. I'll give you a call and let you know when."

"No problem," Mike said, when Kat didn't move. "Just let us know."

The ambulance arrived then, and Mike raised Kat to her feet to get them out of way. He took her into his arms. "It's all right. It's over. Everything will be fine now."

She shook her head silently against his shoulder. *How can it be? I screwed up, royally.*

"Are you okay?" Mike asked, sounding concerned.

She finally found her voice. "I thought Edward was dead . . . and it was all my fault."

"No, it was Joey's fault," Mike said firmly. "He set all of

this in motion, and he pulled the trigger. You can't blame yourself."

Sure I can.

"Hey," Mike said, tipping her face up to his. "At least you didn't run away this time." He gave a sharp laugh. "The one time I wanted you to run away, you ran headfirst into danger."

Duh. Because she had to. But if he was trying to make her feel better, it wasn't working. After the revelation she'd just had, she was going to have to think long and hard about making a few changes in her life.

AS THEY NEARED the police station, Mike worried about Kat. They'd holed up in the B&B until the chief called, and she looked so defeated, so unlike her normally bouncy self. Even Lira seemed concerned—she stuck close to Kat and kept licking her as if to comfort her.

When they got to the station, he held the door for them as Kat trudged into the police station like a zombie. Mike wasn't sure how to get her out of this funk. Maybe this meeting would help.

The chief, Mike, Kat, Edward and Joey—his hands hand-cuffed in front of him now—all crowded into one room. Glad to see Edward up and about, Mike asked him, "How are you doing?"

Edward waved away his concern. "Better. Still a little woozy, but the dosage was set for a dog Lira's size, and, while she's a big dog, she only weighs about half what I do."

"See, I told you," Joey said. "I wasn't going to kill her, just tranq her."

The chief ignored him. "Now, you have two choices," he

said to Edward. "You can take this to trial or settle it here. Which would you prefer?"

Wisely, the man said, "Here," though his irritated glance at his nephew spoke volumes.

"Thank you," Joey said fervently. "You know it was an accident—"

"Hush now," the chief said. "You're not out of the woods yet." Again speaking to Edward, he asked, "Do you want to press charges against your nephew?"

Edward shook his head. "No."

"Against Ms. Channing?"

Edward thought about it for a moment, then glanced warily at Mike. "No."

"No?" Joey exclaimed. "But what about what she did? She kidnapped your dog." He lifted his cuffed hands to point an accusing finger at her. "And she sicced the dog on me. I saw her give the cue." He glanced frantically around the room, looking for support. He didn't get it, but persisted anyway. "That dog could be considered a weapon, right? She used a deadly weapon against me."

Kat snorted and shook her head. Surprisingly, she didn't say anything.

"I'm not going to file charges against Kat," Edward said. "And if you think it through, you'll see why."

"Well, then *I'll* file charges against her," Joey said in triumph, therefore proving that he didn't, in fact, think at all.

Kat winced, but didn't say anything to defend herself.

"Ms. Channing, did you command the dog to attack Mr. Barton?"

"Yes," she said, and a little of her spark came back into her eyes. "And I'd do the same again."

Mike suppressed a grin. Now there was the Kat he loved.

"And why did you give that command?" the chief asked.

"Because I thought he had a real gun, that he had killed Edward and was going to kill Lira. And maybe even me."

"That's ridic—"

"That's enough," the chief told Joey firmly. "You can file charges if you like, Mr. Barton, but, given the circumstances, I don't think anyone would convict her."

Mike noticed he left unsaid the fact that it would be a waste of everyone's time, though his tone certainly implied it. Unfortunately, Joey was stupid enough to do it out of spite.

Joey glared at Kat and opened his mouth, but Edward said sharply, "Drop it. We don't need any more bad press."

Joey looked frustrated, but thankfully did as his uncle said. Mike breathed a sigh of relief. Kat was safe from prosecution.

"It seems you were all guilty of bad judgment," the chief said wryly, glancing at everyone in the room.

Edward's lips grew tight, but he didn't say anything. And his fierce look at Joey kept his nephew's mouth shut as well. Kat just continued to look miserable.

But Mike wouldn't leave it at that. "So, are you going to issue a statement to the press?" he asked Edward.

When the man merely nodded, Mike prodded, "And what are you going to say?"

"I'll say that Lira wasn't kidnapped, that it was all a misunderstanding." He grimaced. "I'll have to explain about her eyesight, and announce her retirement as well, saying she was coming to Sanctuary for a well-deserved rest."

Mike nodded in satisfaction . . . and not a little relief. It looked like everything really was going to be all right.

"Good," the chief said firmly. "I'll hold you to that. And now, for the disposition of the dog."

"Legally, she's mine," Edward said, giving Kat an annoyed glance.

Kat's eyes widened and she looked to Mike for help.

He couldn't resist her silent plea—he had to do something. "But if she's retired, you really have no use for her, do you?" Mike asked.

"Well, she could still do public appearances, promote the movie," Edward said defiantly.

"But wouldn't it look better in the press if you allowed her assistant to adopt her?"

Kat looked hopeful, but Edward frowned. "How could she take care of Lira? She has no job, no place to live . . ."

"She's going to live with me," Mike said firmly, then added, "until she gets on her feet again."

"That won't—"

"Mr. Barton," Chief McPherson interrupted, "I highly recommend you reconsider. It seems like a viable solution."

"But we have a few more scenes she needs to shoot. . . ."

The chief frowned. "I'm not sure I want to release the dog into your custody . . . unless Ms. Channing is there to watch out for her welfare."

Edward sighed. "Okay, okay." He glanced ruefully at Lira. "I don't have time to train another assistant for the few remaining scenes, and Kat already knows her routine. Everyone will understand if we have to cancel Lira's appearances. Plus we've gotten a lot of publicity already with this whole mess."

Mike pressed, "So, you agree to let Kat stay with Lira and adopt her when the movie is over?"

Edward sighed. "Yes."

The joy on Kat's face was all the reward Mike needed.

But Joey wasn't so happy. "You've got to be kidding. You're going to hire her back *and* let her have your biggest asset?"

"Shut up," Edward said with a snarl. "One more word out of you, and *you're* fired, family or not."

Joey's eyes grew wide, but he clamped his lips together.

Good. Maybe they'd stay that way.

"Besides," Edward added, glaring at Kat, "I'm not going to pay you for these past few days, and I figure you owe me the next couple of weeks, no pay."

Mike started to open his mouth to protest, but Kat grabbed his arm. "That's fair," she said.

"Now," Mike said, "there's the matter of all the time and effort the Dogwood police department put into this because of your nephew. I'm sure it cost them a lot of money."

The chief frowned at him. "Are you asking him to reimburse us?"

"No, sir," Mike was quick to assure him, realizing the chief might think he was soliciting a bribe. "I'm saying maybe he could donate something to Sanctuary in Lira's name. She might even become an ambassador for rescued dogs everywhere."

"Good idea," the chief said, "if Mr. Barton is willing."

He raised his hands in capitulation. "Okay, okay. I'll do it."

The chief glanced between Kat and Joey. "And what about you two? What's *your* plan?" When they both obviously had no clue what he was talking about, he added, "What's your plan to atone for the time and trouble you've put everyone through?"

They seemed at a loss, so Mike said, "How about if they donate time to Sanctuary? They can always use volunteers." Before Edward could protest, he added, "After the movie is complete, of course."

Edward nodded with satisfaction. Mike added, "Kat could help with socialization—they'd love to have her do that. And Joey could clean out the kennels." With any luck, they'd have him clean the mouse cages . . . and let Mike watch.

Kat brightened—whether at the thought of Joey doing

scut work or her being able to work with the traumatized dogs, he wasn't sure.

"Hey," Joey protested. At a stern glance from his uncle, he raised his hands. "All right. All right."

"I can do that," Kat said.

The chief smiled. "Good. I'll contact Tad Brightwell so you can make a joint statement." He gave Mike a sidelong look. "Are you sure you're not a Dogwood resident? You sure act like one."

Mike smiled at the huge compliment. "An honorary one, maybe. But I do have to get back to work tomorrow in the Springs."

"Will the practice let you return?" Kat asked.

He shrugged. "I haven't heard otherwise." And he shouldn't, since no one should be the wiser about what had really happened.

Kat chewed her lip, but didn't say anything.

Edward, of course, did. "I'll expect *you* back on the job tomorrow as well," he told Kat.

Kat nodded. "I'll be there."

The chief smiled and rose. "Thank you all for being so reasonable. You're free to go." He glanced significantly at Edward. "But I will let Sanctuary and Tad Brightwell know about the donations of time and money, and I'll help you find someone to start legal paperwork to transfer ownership of Lira to Ms. Channing."

Good man. Mike suppressed a smile at this evidence of the chief's determination to make sure they all followed through on their promises.

"Ownership only," Edward said. "I want it spelled out that she's not entitled to any residuals from Lira's work, and I won't allow her to profit financially from Lira in any way."

Kat beamed. "Deal!"

As the chief removed Joey's handcuffs and did whatever

paperwork was necessary to release him, Mike led Kat out to the car. The difference in her mood was remarkable.

"Wow, you were great in there," Kat enthused. "The donation to Sanctuary, letting me adopt Lira, and having Lira be an ambassador—that was brilliant."

It was nice to see Kat smiling again. Remembering Betsy Mae's advice, Mike thought this might be the right time to discuss how he felt about her. If he could get it past that huge lump in his throat. . . .

But Kat spoke before he could. "We need to head back to your house right away so I can get my car and go back to my trailer."

He paused for a moment. Maybe this wasn't the right time. Oddly, the lump disappeared. "I thought you were staying with me?"

"Well, that was when I thought I didn't have a job. I have to be on site with Lira until she's done shooting her scenes. And I need to find a way to get her hair back to normal, or she won't look like herself—the hair stylist on the set can help with that since it was a temporary dye. Plus I want to get Lira settled, back into a routine."

"I see," Mike said. Didn't she *want* to be with him?

Apparently sensing his less than enthusiastic response, Kat said, "You understand, don't you? The sooner I get this over with, the sooner I can adopt Lira, do my time with Sanctuary, and be free to do whatever I want. Get my life back to normal."

What did that mean? Kat's "normal" wasn't like anyone else's. "You can still stay with me afterward, until you find your way."

"We'll see," she said evasively.

Well, he'd have to live with that . . . for now. But no matter where she ran, he'd find her. Kat was not getting away from him again. Not for long, anyway.

CHAPTER NINETEEN

WHILE LIRA GOT her hair back to normal and filmed her last few scenes over the next two weeks, Kat had a lot of time to think about her life choices . . . about everything. Thanks to Mike, she'd had a very narrow escape from the consequences of her impulsiveness. It had been the most frightening time of her life, and she never wanted to go through that again.

Now that the movie had wrapped, Lira and Kat were no longer needed. Edward had hinted strongly—okay, told her outright—that Kat should vacate the trailer, so she had packed up her few belongings, and she and Lira had headed toward Dogwood where she could do her volunteer time.

Sanctuary was thrilled to have her, and she and Lira had quite a bit of success with the dogs needing socialization over the past week, if she did say so herself. At Kat's suggestion, they'd done some Facebook Live chats with Lira and the shelter pets needing adoption, and the publicity was already successful in bringing in new pet parents.

Though Mike had offered her a room at his house, Kat declined. She told him it was because it was too far to commute, but the truth was, she'd needed to figure things out before she spent any length of time with him again.

She had some savings, enough for a little while, and Betsy Mae had kindly given her a smaller room at the B&B at a reduced rate, and the quaint pink-and-white striped room was oddly comforting and conducive to the kind of deep thinking Kat needed.

Lira nosed her, and she obligingly leaned down to scratch her ears. "Soon, you'll be all mine—legally," she told the sweet dog.

She wanted to provide a good home for the former movie star, but her self-assessment made her understand that the reason she'd never had a pet of her own before was precisely because she was too flighty, too unsettled, too much on the move to take care of one properly. She hated to admit it, but her mother had been right about her.

"But now, I promise I'll be a responsible pet owner," she told Lira. She was determined to be someone Mike would be proud of . . . if he'd have her. He had shown some interest, but was it because he loved her as much as she loved him . . . or had their shared adventure made their flirtation seem more than it really was?

She was fairly certain that had nothing to do with her own feelings. She'd loved Mike as a friend for a very long time, but hadn't noticed when friendship turned into romantic love. In a total "duh" moment, she finally understood that was one of the reasons why her relationships had never worked. She'd always compared other men to Mike . . . and they'd all come up wanting. If she was honest with herself, she'd have to admit that she'd probably sabotaged any relationship that looked as though it was turning serious.

"But do I deserve him?" she asked Lira. The dog licked her hand reassuringly, but Kat was unsure. She had already put some changes into effect to prove to herself—and to him—

that she was worthy of his love. Now she just had to explain it to the man himself and see how he reacted.

Though she'd gotten another cell phone, this wasn't the kind of discussion a responsible person had over the phone. So, since she and Lira—and Mike—had been invited to Sanctuary's annual volunteers' Thanksgiving dinner, she planned to take him aside and talk to him there.

She normally didn't care for Thanksgiving, since it brought back memories of intense family bickering, but maybe this one would be different. "Come on, girl, let's get ready to see Mike again."

She wore one of those pretty sweaters Aimee had bought for her, one that clung to her few curves, and spiffed herself up to look her best. Hoping Mike would appreciate her efforts, she headed for Sanctuary, her stomach churning in anticipation.

She and Lira entered the Sanctuary greeting area which had been cleared out to fit a whole gutload of tables and a ton of delicious-smelling food. Looked like they expected a huge crowd. It was great to see all the volunteers as well as the other Dogwood residents she had come to know. She peered around. Mike wasn't here yet, though.

But they'd certainly been spotted. Lira was a popular addition to any gathering—especially with the children. One little boy came running over and asked, "Can Lira play?"

"Of course."

Lira bounded off joyfully with the boy, and Kat soon heard her signature howl. She made a mental note to limit the number of howls per day, or the poor people of Dogwood would get sick of hearing it.

The sheepdog was adapting well to her vision loss, though she still stayed close to Kat at night. And Edward was true to his word, issuing a statement that said the alleged dognapping was simply a misunderstanding, and providing a hefty donation to the shelter . . . which he publicized, of course. And Joey had promised to start volunteering after Thanksgiving. Thank goodness she wouldn't have to deal with him today.

"Kat Channing?" a woman asked behind her.

Kat turned to see a lovely, professional-looking woman. "Guilty."

The woman laughed and held out her hand. "Hi, I'm Bliss Galore."

"Really? What a great movie star name."

She grimaced. "A porn star, maybe. But I won't have that name for much longer. See that tall, handsome man over there with our border collie mix? That's Luke McPherson, my fiancé."

"So you'll be another McPherson?" There were certainly a lot of them here in Dogwood.

Bliss laughed. "Yeah, I'll be one of many."

"Congratulations," Kat said, wondering why the woman was telling her this.

"But that's not what I want to talk to you about. The chief asked me to help draw up the agreement to allow you to adopt Lira." She smiled. "As of yesterday afternoon, Mr. Barton has agreed and signed it. Lira is now legally yours."

Kat couldn't help it—she threw her arms around the woman. "Oh, wow. This is truly a day for giving thanks."

Bliss hugged her back. "Normally, I wouldn't discuss work on a holiday, but I figured you'd like to know."

"I do. Thank you so much!"

"You're very welcome. Now I'd better go tend to my fiancé. Nice to meet you."

"You, too," Kat said.

A man spoke behind her. "Hello, stranger."

She whirled. "Mike!" Whoa—he looked different. He'd

started growing a beard. She'd never seen him this way. But who cared? It was her Mike.

She hugged him quickly, lingering longer than she should have. It felt so good to hold him again, but until they clarified what their relationship really was, she wasn't going to push it.

"Can we talk?" he asked.

He wanted to do this *now*? Well, why not? "Okay." She glanced around at the hubbub. "Maybe somewhere out of the way?"

"Sure. Follow me."

As they headed toward a door at the opposite end of the room, a number of other people stopped to greet them, so it took a while to get there, but they did, finally. Mike opened the door to Paul's office, and motioned for Kat to precede him.

She did, and, after he closed the door, he gave her an appraising look. "You look great," he said, his gaze taking in the curves revealed beneath her sweater.

Glad her hard work had produced such positive results, Kat grinned. "You look pretty good yourself. But what's with the beard?"

"I thought I'd try something different." He stroked it, then posed with a raised eyebrow. "You like it?"

"I don't know yet," she answered truthfully. It was so very different. Kinda scruffy, but kinda sexy, too.

He took her hands in his. "So, when are you coming to stay with me?"

"Oh, Mike, I really appreciate your willingness to have me there, but I don't want to put you out."

"You wouldn't be putting me out. You know I have lots of room."

But she couldn't do that and follow through with her

plan. "I'm sorry, Mike." She took a deep breath. "I've come to a decision and want to let you know what it is."

His face fell. "You're running again?"

"No, just the opposite. I'm moving to Dogwood. Permanently." Before he could say anything, she rushed into her explanation. "I love it here, and though Betsy Mae has been wonderful in giving me a special room rate, I need a place of my own." At a howl from the other room, she grinned. "And so do Lira and Samson."

"The little Chihuahua?"

"Yes—he and Lira have become great friends, and I fell in love with the little guy. As soon as I have a house with a yard, I'll adopt him."

"Can you afford a house?"

"Yes—Paul and Sandy have offered me a job. Lira has brought so much positive attention to Sanctuary that they want me to help with coordinating the Facebook Live videos and other social media, plus coordinate all the new volunteers. And . . . I'm working with Dogwood Realty to buy a house." She peered at him to see his reaction.

Oddly, his smile widened. "You are? That's quite a big decision."

"Yes, I figure it's about time I settled down, became less impulsive, more responsible."

He laughed. "Not *too* much, I hope."

"What?" She was doing this for him—didn't he realize that?

He shook his head. "I know I've berated you for your impulsiveness, but it's one of the things I love about you."

Did he really just say the "L" word? "You—you do?"

"Yes. You were right about me—you made me realize how stuck in a rut I was. You make life fun, adventurous, worth living. I was a fool to tell you not to be yourself."

"But I'm trying to show you how responsible I've

become," she protested. "You've always been the steady one, the one I could count on." That's what *she* loved about *him*.

"Well, I still am, but I've made a few changes myself." He stroked his chin. "The beard is one of them, and I have a secret to tell you." He leaned in and whispered, "My soup cans are all mixed up with the cereal boxes."

For a moment, she was thrown for a loop, then remembered her assertion that he'd never be able to have disorder in his pantry. She laughed. "So, it looks like we're good for each other, doesn't it?"

"It does. And I need to tell you . . . I'm looking for a place to live in Dogwood, too."

"You are?" He'd be nearby? How wonderful!

"Yes, I've given my notice at the practice in Colorado Springs, and I plan to join one here."

"You're really leaving the home you grew up in?" Maybe he *had* changed. Not that he needed to. Not for her.

"Yes, why not? It's just a house. Besides, I was hoping . . . maybe we can buy one together?"

As she stared at him, shocked, he inexplicably pulled out his phone and texted someone.

Puzzled, she asked, "What was that about?"

"You'll see," he said mysteriously. "So, want to buy a house together?"

"I don't know." That depended on a lot of things. She couldn't be just his roommate and best friend. She wanted to ask him what he'd meant by "love," but was too cowardly to bring it up herself. Instead, she asked obliquely, "So . . . why are you moving here?"

"Well, for one thing, I love this town, just as much as you do. And they need more veterinarians here—the ratio of animals to humans is much higher in Dogwood than anywhere else in the state."

"You're not moving to be near Amber?" She mentally crossed her fingers. *Please say no. Please say no.*

He looked puzzled for a moment, then said, "She's not in the picture. It's you I love, Kat. It's always been you."

Adrenaline flooded through her, filling her with relief. Could it be true? "I—"

A knock came at the door, and though Kat wanted to ignore it and explore this *very* interesting topic, Mike said, "Just on time."

He opened the door to show Bliss on the other side. She grinned and let her border collie in, then closed the door. The cute dog looked up at Mike, an obvious question on her face. Kat knew how she felt. What the heck was going on? *Let's get back to the I love you's, please!*

"Do you know who this is?" Mike asked.

"It's Bliss's dog."

"Yes, that, and you see that heart-shaped splotch on her side?"

"Yes." Then added, "Oh." The town legend.

"This is Match. That heart shape shows that she's the town's newest matchmaking dog, and she's very good at her job." Gazing down at Match, he asked, "Match, is Kat my one true love?"

Kat held her breath as the dog cocked her head, considering them for a moment. Then she ran in tight circles around them, looking up at them expectantly. What was she trying to say? Was she trying to herd them together? Or freak them out so they jumped apart?

Kat wasn't sure until Match got impatient at Kat's cluelessness and suddenly jumped up, shoving her forepaws against Kat's behind, and pushed her into Mike's arms.

She fell willingly and looked up at Mike with a smile.

"You see?" Mike said softly, stroking her cheek. "Match thinks we should be together—and Match is never wrong."

"I finally believe. . . ." Kat breathed. But she didn't need Match to confirm the fact that they belonged together.

"I hoped you would. So, will you marry me?"

Joy filled her. Who else should she marry but her best friend?

"Oh, Mike, I love you too. . . ." But she had to hesitate.

"What's wrong?" Mike asked, his brow furrowed. "Are you worried that our marriage will turn out like your parents'? That will *never*—"

She put a finger on his lips. "No, I'm not worried about that. Not anymore. I know I'm nothing like my mother, and you're nothing like my father. We'd probably be more like *your* parents." She remembered their loving relationship from her childhood.

"Then what's wrong?"

"Nothing, really." She gave him a saucy look. "I just didn't want you to think I was too impulsive if I said yes immediately."

He threw back his head and laughed. "So is that a yes?"

"It's a yes," she confirmed.

"Finally," he breathed, and leaned down to claim her lips with his.

Match barked and leapt with excitement at this evidence of another true match in Dogwood.

Best. Thanksgiving. Ever.

Dear Reader,

The idea for this series came about when my critique group got together at a Romance Writers of America conference one year. We decided to write a series together, and since we all love animals and know Colorado very well, Dogwood was born.

Thank you so much for coming along for the ride from Colorado Springs to Dogwood. I hope you enjoyed reading it as much as I did writing it!

And if you did, please share your love for the Dogwood Series by leaving a review, even if it's only a sentence or two! Your reviews make a ton of difference and are so appreciated.

Monthly Prize Drawing

The series authors will donate goodies to a monthly Dogwood Delights box, including such things as signed books and fun pet-related items. We will draw one name at random from subscribers to our monthly newsletter, the *Dogwood Digest*, so if you want to be considered, sign up at DogwoodSeries.com/monthly-prize-drawing/

Learn More

Visit our Website at DogwoodSeries.com
Join our Facebook Group at
Facebook.com/groups/dogwooddevotee/

And, in appreciation for the work done by animal rescue organizations, each author will donate a portion of all sales to one of them. Thanks for reading!

Pam McCutcheon
Colorado Springs, CO

DOGWOOD SERIES BOOKS

These are in order of publication, but may be read as stand-alones in any order.

A Match in Dogwood, a Dogwood Romance Prequel
Anthology with seven authors

Chasing Bliss, a Dogwood Romantic Comedy
by Jodi Anderson

Sit. Stay. Love., a Dogwood Romantic Comedy
by Pam McCutcheon
(July 2018)

Love at First Bark, a Dogwood Sweet Romance
by Jude Willhoff
(August 2018)

Must Love Dogs, a Dogwood Sweet Romance
by Karen Fox
(September 2018)

Second Chance Ranch, a Dogwood Sweet Romance
by Sharon Silva
(October 2018)

Welcome Home, Soldier, a Dogwood Sweet Romance

by Angel Smits

(November 2018)

A Dogwood Christmas, a Dogwood anthology

(December 2018)

Doggone, a Dogwood Romantic Comedy

by Laura Hayden

(January 2019)

ACKNOWLEDGMENTS

I would like to thank Buddy Mandeville, DVM, for answering all my questions about the dog and horse medical conditions. Any mistakes are mine alone.

And, as always, thanks to my critique group and fellow Dogwood series authors Jodi Anderson, Karen Fox, Laura Hayden, Sharon Silva, Angel Smits, and Jude Willhoff. It's been a blast working with you!

ABOUT THE AUTHOR

 Pam McCutcheon is the award-winning author of romance novels ranging from fantasy, futuristic, paranormal, and time travel to contemporary romantic comedy. She also has fantasy short stories and two nonfiction how-to books for writers in print, and writes the Demon Underground New Adult urban fantasy series under the name Parker Blue.

After many years of working for the military as enlisted, officer, and civil service successively, she left her industrial engineering position to pursue her first love—a career as a writer. She lives in beautiful Colorado Springs with her rescue dog.

Contact her at:
www.pammc.com
pammc@pcisys.net

🇫